HOME FOR CHRISTMAS

MADDIE JAMES

HOME FOR CHRISTMAS

A Dickens Holiday Romance

Maddie James

Sign up here for news of contests, giveaways, and new releases.

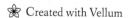 Created with Vellum

HOME FOR CHRISTMAS

A star-crossed, holiday romance story of young love, old love, holding on, and letting go.

During the summer of 1989, Jenny Anderson meets Ben Matthews during a beach vacation with their families. Fresh out of high school and ready to get on with life—Jenny to Penn State in the fall and Ben to work for his uncle at Dickens Hardware—they didn't expect to fall in love.

But *love-at-first-sight* happens anyway.

This long-distance relationship doesn't deter them. After a summer of love letters and clandestine trips in the fall, Ben asks Jenny's father for her hand in marriage over Thanksgiving weekend. Much to Jenny's horror, her father angrily denies his request.

That's when Ben and Jenny devise a plan to elope, enjoy a Christmas honeymoon in the mountains, and settle into life in the Christmas Village of Dickens. Jenny hopes her parents will come around, finally give their blessing, and welcome Ben into the family.

But plans go awry when Ben's truck breaks down not far out of Dickens. The young couple takes refuge from a fast-approaching snowstorm at an old farmhouse with elderly occupants. The pause in their getaway causes Jenny to have doubts—until she witnesses first-hand the power of love and the magic of Christmas.

ONE

J enny Anderson shoved her backpack through her bedroom window and peered out over her parents' front lawn. The bag was a lot fuller than she had expected, since she'd tucked a couple of Christmas gifts inside at the last minute—but she'd manage. The night was crisp, clear, with a near-full moon shining down from behind the house, casting shadows and dancing light across the neighborhood. She'd waited for the old grandfather clock in their entryway to chime midnight, then made her move.

She felt rather silly, honestly, sneaking out of the house. She was an adult, for goodness' sake—she turned nineteen-years-old in October. But here she was, sneaking all the same, and avoiding the inevitable confrontation with her parents.

In particular, her father.

The backpack tumbled and slid a few feet down the incline of the steep porch roof, making a snake trail in the skiff of snow

1

on the shingles. One leg through the window, followed by the other, Jenny sat on the edge and studied her surroundings, wondering how many of her neighbors had seen their Philadelphia neighborhood from this vantage point.

She didn't worry about the house alarm. The security lock on this window had never worked. She'd discovered that years ago, and of course, had not divulged that information to her parents. She'd snuck out on occasion during her teen years. Tonight, it made her escape easier than walking out the front door, avoiding disarming the alarm and waking her parents.

It was a pretty view up here, she decided. Serene. She took a moment to gather into herself, knowing that this peaceful feeling might be her last one for a while—that is, until she and Ben got on their way, and she had a wedding ring on her finger. Until then, she'd likely be a nervous wreck.

But right now, sitting in the dark, high above everything but the treetops, she breathed in frosty air and welcomed the silence and the tranquility. Inhaling deep, she sighed, letting the breath out long and slow.

She'd like to freeze this moment in time—just for a few minutes. The previous few weeks had been too stressful with all the family drama. Up here, on the roof, things were simpler and, well, nice.

Calm before the storm?

She didn't want to consider another storm. She was ready for peace.

And she was ready for Ben.

The lights twinkled on the fresh-fallen snow, winking between the branches. The streetlights provided a soft, blueish glow to the tree-lined street. Tastefully trimmed for the season, the colonial houses of her neighborhood sported candles in the windows, and traditional wreaths on the doors, with spotlights shining up on them from the lawn. Christmas trees sparkled in the windows of a few dark houses. And to her left, her closest neighbors, the Garrison's, went all out with a Santa and sleigh on their roof.

"Well, hello there, Santa," she whispered. "Fancy meeting you up here."

Scooting off the sill, she turned to lower the window. Carefully. Simultaneously, her sock snagged at the ankle on a nail sticking out from the roof.

"Shoot," she whispered, plucking at the sock and tearing a hole in it. Oh well, she'd change it later. Closing the window with a soft click, she sat on the cold asphalt shingles. Exhaling, she shivered and snatched at the backpack, scooting her way to the edge of the roof, and the ivy-heavy trellis attached to the side porch.

She'd done this a dozen times or so—snuck out after her parents were fast asleep—but this time was different. Her previous excursions were because she was a semi-rebellious teenager, tired of curfews and her parents' disapproving notions about all her friends, and what she should, or should not, be doing on a Saturday night.

Now, her sneaking out seemed ridiculous. She should have simply told them she was leaving and walked out the front door —but that seemed logical.

And nothing, lately, was logical.

By daybreak, she expected to be in the small-town Christmas Village of Dickens in New England—with Ben, the love of her life.

Breathing deep, she exhaled. *Her Ben.*

It was the right thing to do—for her and for Ben. She had a good head on her shoulders. She'd graduated high school with honors in May and was now a freshman in college. She was smart, and she knew what she wanted in life. She was acting in her own best interest—living her life how she wanted. What she wasn't doing was deciding blindly, as her father may have suggested a couple of weeks earlier.

She and Ben had thought it through.

She was ready to push herself from the nest—just not in the direction her parents wanted.

For them, college followed by law school was her future, and then a position in her dad's law firm. Her parents had worked hard and created healthy college funds for her and her older sister, Candy. That they would graduate from a university, and continue to graduate school, had always been the expectation.

But it wasn't Jenny's dream.

In time, she would get that degree. But when she did, it would be on her own terms, with her own dime, and in her own time. And she would study art, not law. The money her parents had saved for her college would be a nice nest egg for them. She loved her parents—not that she didn't. They'd been good to her growing up, if not overly protective and stricter than the parents of most of her friends. She didn't want to appear disrespectful at all. She just wanted to live her own life, make her own decisions.

Her father had made that impossible with his demands and ultimatums. She knew that living her life to please her father was neither healthy for her, nor in her best interest. He'd basically forced her hand on the issue and her mother had gone along with him.

A letter she'd left behind explained her plans, where she was going, who she was with. She'd call them later. After.

Maybe they could take some of that college money and do something nice for themselves. She hoped so. They rarely took time off from work to spend time together. Perhaps they could take that cruise they've bantered about for years.

It made her happy to think about that.

The thing she knew for certain, though, was that Penn State and a Philadelphia law firm were not her destiny.

Ben was her future, and tonight, she was going for it.

Vehicle lights rounded the corner at the end of the street. She watched as the older model red pickup truck drove slowly and approached the front of her house. Scooting toward the edge of the roof and the trellis, Jenny slid the backpack over her right shoulder and slipped over the side to climb down the trellis.

Her stomach erupted in a tumble of nervous and happy butterflies.

Ben stopped his truck at the end of her driveway, killed his headlights, and kept the engine running.

She reached the ground running toward the truck.

TWO

SIX MONTHS EARLIER, June 1989

Ben Matthews tossed another sideways glance at the girl in the pink bikini with the sheer white coverup as she strolled down the shore. He'd watched her for the past fifteen minutes as she made her way back up the beach. Pausing in front of his house, she stooped to pick up something in the sand, glanced his way, then righted herself and wandered on. A stiff breeze raced off the ocean, swirling her long hair around her head and teasing at the coverup, playing peek-a-boo with flashes of pink and tanned skin.

Ben shifted and stood, watching her, his twenty-year-old libido getting the best of him.

It wasn't the first time he'd seen her. She'd caught his eye the morning he and his family arrived at their beach rental. Seemed they both were earlier risers—he liked to watch the sunrise from the rambling front porch of the beach house with a cup of coffee, and she liked to walk the shore and pick up pretty little objects—rocks and glass and shells, he assumed.

Truth was, this was the third morning he'd watched her, and he wondered why he'd not yet introduced himself. Summer beach week only lasts so long, right? Why waste time?

He set the coffee mug on the wooden deck rail.

Now or never.

As he strolled down the boarded walkway leading away from the house, his mind drifted, but his gaze still flicked back and forth to her. He was glad about this vacation week with his parents. His job responsibilities working for his uncle would gear-up soon, after they returned home, and he wasn't sure when he'd get another week off. Until he graduated from high school a semester early last year, he'd worked at the hardware store part-time—evenings, weekends, and summers. This past eighteen months, he'd worked full time. And in a couple of weeks, he'd take over as the manager. He was looking forward to an increased paycheck and was glad to have the work in the family business, especially now that his uncle was talking about retirement.

His future was bright, and he was grateful for that.

One day Dickens Hardware would be his.

Not sure why his head went there now, he shook off the thoughts. Perhaps looking at the young woman made him think about the future—work, eventual marriage, kids. He wanted that one day. He'd always dreamed of a family. So far, though, none of the girls he'd dated in Dickens held his interest long enough to think about courting one for a long-term deal.

And he really didn't want to think about Dickens Hardware, back in New England, right now. He wanted to fixate on the girl ambling ahead of him on the beach—the pretty brunette who just stooped to pick at something in the sand.

He continued walking. She plucked up an object with her

7

forefinger and studied it, a waterfall of shiny coppery-brown hair sliding over one shoulder.

"What have you got there?"

She looked up and Ben was suddenly awestruck by her eyes—round as sand dollars, deep brown with gold flecks. She held his gaze for several seconds, while his heart kicked up a cadence and every inch of his breath exited his lungs.

He grew a little dizzy.

She batted her long lashes twice and slowly stood.

Ben thought he might pass out from lack of oxygen.

"Hi. I, uh…" She looked at her sandy fingertips where she held a small piece of blue glass. "Sea glass, I think. See?" She held out her hand.

Ben thought his chest might explode with pent-up energy inside that he didn't know what to do with. He took a deep breath, felt a little steadier, and exhaled.

She reached for his hand—small sparks zinging up to his elbow when she did—and laid the sandy object in his palm. Her fingertips lingered over his.

Ben lifted his gaze to look into her eyes again. "I think you're right. It's sea glass." He hadn't even really looked at it.

"I've been collecting all week."

"I know."

"You know?"

"Well…" Ben looked away and shuffled his feet in the sand. "I've seen you."

She said nothing, but the hint of a smile raced across her lips.

"I'm not a stalker," he blurted out.

Her puffy lips stretched into a smile then. "I've seen you, too. Was wondering when you'd come off that porch."

Grinning, and silently relieved, he handed the sea glass back to her. "For your collection."

But she folded his fingers around it. "Keep it. Maybe you'll think of me next time you see it."

She turned and took a few steps toward her beach rental, two doors down from his, pausing once to glance over her shoulder and send him a teasing grin. He stood there soaking up every bit of her lingering gaze until she swiveled back and jogged toward the beach house, while he stared after her like a needy puppy craving attention.

Palming the glass in his hand, he shoved it into his pocket. Somehow, he didn't think he needed the sea glass to remember her.

J enny's heart pounded as she rushed up the wind-and-salt battered steps of the beach house and crossed the porch. As she opened the wooden screen door to slip inside, she glanced down the beach to where the boy was crossing the walkway, two houses down.

She had finally lured him off that deck. After two days, it was about time. He looked her way and Jenny ducked into the house, not wanting him to know that she was watching him, too.

"Finally meet porch boy?" Her sister, Candy, looked up from her magazine. She sat in an overstuffed chair upholstered with a beachy fabric of turquoise shells and seahorses. It was a bit much, to Jenny's liking anyway, but screamed vacation beach rental.

"None of your business." She headed for the stairwell.

"What's his name?"

Well, shoot. Neither one of them shared names. Did they?

"I didn't ask."

Candy stood, the magazine dropping to the chair. "Oh, my God. You didn't even get his name?"

Jenny shrugged, tossing off her response. "No biggie. I'm sure we'll run into each other again. I'm headed for the shower."

Candy rolled her eyes. "Whatever."

Jenny took a couple of steps up the stairs, smiling. Yes, they would run into each other again. She was sure of it. She'd *make* sure of it. No boy had ever looked at her like he did—that deep, longing, satisfying, and fulfilling stare that made her heart nearly jump out of her chest, and sent icy shivers all the way to her toes on this hot summer day. Not to mention the spark that traveled from her fingertips to her core when she'd touched him. That had nearly taken her breath away—and the sensation had taken her quite by surprise.

Sighing, Jenny reached the landing and stripped off her coverup.

She might just marry that boy.

Hours later, the sand crabs scrambling as the last shred of light in the day dissipated, Ben made his way down to the surf for a late walk. Flashlight in hand, he played the light over the beach in front of him, watching for the critters. As he moved closer to the girl's rental, he paused and looked up, and heard loud voices.

"I'll only be gone a minute, Daddy." It was the girl from earlier.

"Jennifer, I'm warning you." Her father? Obviously. His voice was gruff. So, her name was Jennifer. "Don't make this worse than it is," the man added.

"But you told us we'd be here until Friday."

"Things change, honey. We have to go."

The light on the porch backlit the pair, and Ben watched as she turned and faced the beach. Had she seen his flashlight?

"I'll be right back!" She tossed the words over her shoulder, tripping down the steps of the house and onto the sand. Obviously, she paid little attention to the sand crabs—but they skedaddled in her wake. Ben lifted the light to make a path for her, hoping she was coming for him.

Toward him, he corrected himself. Because yes, she was coming his way. Making a direct beeline. For him. To his heart?

"Hey!"

She rushed closer, almost too close, and he caught the glimmer in her eyes and the faint scent of her shampoo. Lemon.

"I hoped I'd see you," she added.

"Hey there. What are you doing?"

"Came out to catch you," she said, then her face lit up with a grin. Out of breath, she paused for a moment, and danced back and forth in the sand on bare feet.

"You're brave," he said.

"Why?"

Ben pointed to her toes. "Crabs."

"Oh!" She hopped a little more and snickered. "They don't scare me."

Ben liked this fearless girl. "Like I said, brave!"

She glanced back to the porch and Ben followed her gaze. Her father still stood there, watching. Turning back, she said, "We're leaving tomorrow. Daddy must get back to work. Some emergency, or something. Who knows? Anyway, I...."

Suddenly, she turned shy on him, glancing away. The half-bashful, half-embarrassed look was charming. She took another deep breath and blew it out.

"Anyway," she started again, making eye contact, "I couldn't go without knowing your name. I'm Jenny."

That's progress. Names were good. "I'm Ben. Ben Matthews."

"Jenny Anderson. Where are you from?"

"Oh, up in New England."

She frowned. "I'm from Philadelphia."

Ben shrugged it off. "Better than Oregon." Maybe a few hours drive for him. Heck, what was he thinking?

"True."

Her father barked her name and she jerked toward the beach house.

"Coming, Dad!"

Looking at Ben, she said, "Goodness. I'm eighteen and going to college in the fall but he still wants to *daddy* me."

"I imagine he always will," Ben told her.

She nodded. "Perhaps."

"Jennifer!"

But instead of paying attention to her father and moving away, she crowded up closer to him. Ben's thoughts went haywire, and he feared his body might implode. This girl—this Jenny—was exciting and energetic and pretty and well... He wouldn't mind if she crowded up even closer.

Or whispered in his ear, like it appeared she was about to do. Her warm breath fanned out across his cheek. "Meet me at the pier at midnight? Can you sneak away?" She pulled back, her eyes big and expectant.

All Ben could do was nod his head and say, "Sure. Midnight."

"Good." Grinning widely, she leaned in and placed a kiss on his cheek. "Good."

Then she ran away again, this Jenny, giggling and tossing an occasional glance over her shoulder, while her father braced himself with his hands on the porch rail of the house, still watching.

"Midnight," he whispered, and glanced at his watch. Two hours.

An eternity.

Jenny's knees were literally knocking. There were still plenty of people milling about at the pier, and she wasn't frightened at all, even though it was late, but her insides were twittery and jumpy. It wasn't chilly out either, so that wasn't it. The June night was balmy and pleasant. Yet, she wanted to hug herself to keep her teeth from chattering.

She stood on the pier, waiting for Ben. A half-moon shone behind her, casting a faint triangular beam from the horizon to the shore, and nicely lighting up the area. Of course, most of the pier lights were still on, too, and the lights from the houses.

She'd snuck out early so she would have plenty of time to quietly get out of the house and make her way several beach houses north. Most of the pier was closed off this time of night, but she stood near the steps looking out over the shallow waters and sand, watching. She'd been sure her parents would be in bed by now when she left, but they were still up packing and cleaning out the refrigerator when she'd sneaked out the back door.

That, was partially why she was nervous. The other reason was because of Ben, and how he had made her feel this afternoon.

She'd done nothing like this before—be boldly defiant of her father—but something told her she couldn't let the opportunity to see Ben one more time slip away. She had to get to know him a little better before she left.

"Jenny?"

She turned, and he approached from the opposite direction

she had expected. He stood there, hands shoved into the pockets of his baggie swim trunks. A light from the pier illuminated his face, and the stiff ocean breeze blew his shaggy dark brown hair away from his forehead.

"Hi, Ben."

He stepped up. "Hey."

"You came."

"Yep. I wanted to."

"Why?" She looked to the deck of the pier, then back up again. "I mean, you must think I'm crazy asking you to meet me here. We've barely even met."

Ben shook his head and moved in tighter. His hand searched for one of hers, found it, and he tugged her closer. As he leaned in, Jenny's outward nervousness subsided, sending all her butterflies skidding off to her belly. She looked up into his face—feeling so drawn to him—wondering what his next move was going to be, waiting.

He whispered. "I need to give you something."

"Oh?"

Nodding, he nuzzled his face next to hers and left a soft, lingering kiss on her cheek. "You left an unanswered kiss behind."

Jenny pulled back. "I did?"

"Um-hm. I decided to give it back."

"But maybe I wanted you to keep it?" She was feeling bold, and obviously, he was too. That made her insides happy and her heart full.

"Did you?"

She felt herself grinning. "I did. Hey. Want to take a walk?"

Easing back a bit, Ben smiled broadly and took her hand. "I'd like that."

They left the pier and walked north, away from the beach houses where they were staying, settling on the steps of a walkover leading to an unoccupied house. Nestled there, sitting shoulder-to-shoulder between the dunes, they faced the ocean and watched the surf roll in. Ben still held Jenny's hand.

"What do you do in Pennsylvania, Jenny." He looked at her and smiled, then glanced back to the ocean, waiting for her response.

She studied him. She liked his smile. One corner of his mouth hiked up a little higher than the other. "I'm working a summer job at a craft store. I start next week. I'm heading to Penn State in the fall."

He turned back her way. "Wow. Impressive."

She shrugged. "It's what my parents want."

"What do you want?"

"Honestly?"

"Sure."

"I'd rather they save the college money or blow it on themselves. I'd rather draw or paint or throw pots. I'm an artist."

"Really?"

"Yes. I have this need to create stuff all the time. The more I do, the better I get."

"But they want you to get a college degree."

"Yes. Except, Dad wants me to major in something besides art. Pre-law."

"But you don't want to?"

She shook her head. "No, I want to set up a small studio. It's not going to happen though."

Ben's gaze caught hers and held, and she sensed he was really listening to her. "Because your parents think a degree in something besides art will serve you better in the long run."

"Yeah." She nodded. "Dad wants me to follow in his footsteps. Join the law firm he founded back home. It's just not me."

"And art is you. I get it."

Jenny paused and searched Ben's eyes. He was genuinely interested in her. "I think you do get it."

A half-grin crossed his face. "Yes, but sort of the opposite. My parents were on the college bandwagon too last year when I graduated. I finished my senior year early and they thought it would be a great idea for me to get a jump on college and get some courses out of the way. But I convinced them they needed me in the family business more than I needed to go to college."

"Oh?"

He nodded. "Yes. I run the family hardware store up in Dickens. You know, the famous New England Christmas village? The hardware store has been in the family for about eighty years now. My uncle has been running it for a couple of decades, but he's close to retirement. I'll inherit it one day."

Jenny thought for a moment. "I think I've heard of Dickens!"

Laughing, Ben tipped his head closer. "Probably. It's been on TV a few times and featured in magazines."

"What a lovely place to live."

Ben squeezed her hand tighter and shifted, gazing into her eyes. "Yes, it is. Perhaps you can visit sometime."

Suddenly, Jenny wanted to, very much. "Maybe so," she whispered. "I would like that."

The butterflies that had balled themselves up in her tummy took flight as Ben leaned in to give her a kiss—this time, on her lips. When his arms went around her and held her tight, she felt warm and safe and, well, as impossible as it sounded, kind of loved.

He broke the kiss and pulled back a little, staring into her eyes. With a forefinger, he brushed a few wayward strands of her hair away from her eyes, his fingers lingering at her temple.

His words came on a whisper. "I rarely do this—kiss a girl this quickly after meeting her. But, Jenny, I feel so drawn to you."

Gazing into his eyes, Jenny felt his sincerity. "I know. Me too. I feel the same."

"You're leaving tomorrow?"

"Yes. I'm afraid so."

"Can I get your number? Address? Can we keep in touch?"

Jenny's heart sang out with joy. Yes! "I would like that very much."

Ben gently kissed her lips again, then whispered, "Good. Me too."

THREE

SEPTEMBER, Penn State

J enny pushed through her dorm room door, crossed the room, and let her heavy backpack slide off her shoulder and onto the bed. She followed the trajectory of the bag with her body, plopping onto the mattress, kicking off her shoes, and throwing an arm over her forehead.

"Long day at the office?"

Her roommate, Claire Beacon, whom she met the first day she moved into her dorm at Penn, asked from across the room where she sat on her own bed.

Jenny kept her eyes closed and blew out a quick breath. "Yeah. Sort of. Headache."

"You know this is not what you want to do, Jenny."

"I know that."

"It's tearing you up inside."

Claire was right. She'd known her for a few short weeks, and already she got her. Just like Ben had gotten her so quickly.

Sitting up, she looked at her roommate. "I know. I would love to go to the pottery studio, but I simply don't have the energy. Algebra and World History and that stupid Psych class are seriously stifling my creative muse."

"Then get out of it."

Jenny shook her head. "Can't."

"Then just wallow in it, I guess. I don't know what else to tell you." Claire rose and headed for her closet, pulling out a sweater. "I'm off to the library." She hooked her arm through a backpack strap. "Oh, I picked up the mail downstairs. You have a letter."

Jenny's mood suddenly lifted. She hopped up. "Thanks!"

Claire smiled. "Now, there's the Jenny we all know and love. Your face lights up when you think of Ben. You need to re-examine your priorities, girl."

Jenny barely paid attention to Claire's leaving as she picked up the letter with the Dickens Christmas postmark sitting on her dresser. Her heart sung with the anticipation of reading Ben's words.

*D*ear Jenny,
  I miss you! I hope your classes are going well, even though I know you dread them. Just hang in there and get through the semester. Maybe things will take a turn for the better as we get closer to the holidays.

Speaking of the holidays, we are already gearing up here for Christmas in Dickens at the hardware. We've started stocking up on Christmas lights and decorations, because we know as people get into their attics and drag down their decorations, they discover broken lights and frayed cords and then they all head over here for supplies. We are coming up on our busiest season of the year and I need to be ready!

Uncle Herb is not doing so well, and he's stepped back to only working one day a week now. I'm loving managing the store and know this was what I was meant to do but I miss having him around. He is such a wealth of knowledge about hardware in general, but also about the history of the old place and the community. I feel I should carry that on, for the family and for the town. I have a lot of ideas for the future. I can't wait to show you the store when you visit. Are you still planning to get away for fall break in early October? I will come get you. I've mapped it out. It will take me about seven hours to get to you. Let me know!

I love you, Jenny. I miss you so much. Hope to hear from you soon. I will call you on Saturday, like normal.

Love,

Ben

Jenny lowered the letter, tears in her eyes, and sighed. She loved and missed Ben. How this had all happened so quickly, she would never know, but she was happy it had. She and Ben truly fell in love at first sight that day on the beach last summer.

She'd not been looking forward to her days at Penn State —not at all—but meeting Ben, and their summer letters and phone calls, had helped her to wrap her brain around the idea. They'd also managed one brief meeting in the summer, in late August, before she headed off to college. She'd told her parents she was going on a day shopping splurge for college things with her friend, Pam, but drove a couple of hours to meet Ben at a state park in northeastern Pennsylvania.

They'd picnicked and hiked the trails, but mostly just enjoyed holding hands, talking, and being together. It was during that day that Jenny knew she was over-the-moon in love with Ben.

And that was the day he'd told her he loved her, too.

He'd helped soften the blow about college somewhat, too, that day, and encouraged her to do her best for now, to give it a try. It was his idea to find some place in State College where she could do her art, and she'd loved him for that. If she could only make time to get there. He understood, but he knew she was unhappy, deep down.

She also knew he didn't want their relationship to be the reason she didn't succeed at college. That was why he wanted her to hang in there and complete the semester.

Even though she was miserable.

Jenny gazed out the window over the campus with unseeing eyes, then heaved a thick sigh. She wasn't happy here, and one day she was going to have to break it to her parents. But as Ben said, the best thing she could do now was finish out the semester and go from there. That was her plan.

In the meantime, she'd write to him and visit. The thought of seeing him in just a couple of weeks made her insides giddy with happiness and contentment.

Dear Ben,

I miss you too! I can't wait to see you and to see Dickens. I've heard so much about it I have pictures in my head. Now, I'll soon see it all for myself. I wonder if Dickens really looks like what I think it does? Seven hours is a long trip for you to make one way and turn around to drive back. And then to bring me back to college again! Should we come up with a different plan? Would it be better if I took a bus to Dickens? Maybe even part of the way?

I wish Dad would let me have my car here, but he won't budge on that. Not until I'm a sophomore. He didn't let my sister have her car her freshman year, either.

I've never taken a bus outside of the city, but I can look into it. What do you think? We can talk about it on Saturday. You may not get this letter before we talk, though.

You always make me feel better when I get your letters. I was having a rough day today, then your letter perked me up. I have to be honest, though. I really dislike my classes. I feel I'm wasting precious time. I am tired and don't feel like going to the studio at the end of the day. But I *need* to do those things occasionally, so I can remember who I am.

Geez, sorry for the downer. I'm fine. I truly am. I'm just so happy we are going to see each other soon. I can't wait to see Dickens and the hardware store and the gazebo and everything else you've told me about. I think I am already in love with the town, just as much as I love you. Talk soon, Ben.

Love you bunches,
Jenny

FOUR

"Jennifer, this is not a good idea. We really don't know these people. It's dangerous."

"Mom, it's Ben. I'm staying with his family."

Staring out her dorm window, Jenny listened to her mother drone on about all the reasons she should not go to Dickens for fall break. Her voice prattled in the wings of her brain while Jenny pulled back the curtains and watched for Ben's truck to pull up to the sidewalk.

The day was Friday, and the sun was just barely poking its head up in the east. Claire was in the shower, singing loudly. Jenny had cleared her classes for the day, turning in all her assignments early, and didn't have to be back on campus until a week from Monday.

She'd been responsible when making her plans. Mostly. But none of that seemed to matter to her parents.

"This makes me very uncomfortable, Jennifer. We only

have your best interest in mind. What I don't understand is why you are not coming home for fall break? We would love to see you."

"I'm coming home for Thanksgiving. We already talked about that, right? Most people stay on campus during fall break. I'm just going to Dickens to see Ben. It's not a big deal."

"Well, I don't like it."

"Well, I suppose I could stay on campus and party my ass off all week, instead. Would you like that any better?"

"Jennifer!"

Jenny blew out a breath, stepped closer to the window, and peered down the street. That comment was probably out of line —probably nothing. It was out of line. But her mother was being ridiculous.

Time was ticking away, and she expected Ben soon. He couldn't get here fast enough. Her stomach was suddenly in knots, her insides jittery. She searched the traffic for his red truck—a 1980 Ford F100 pickup, he'd told her once—like that would mean anything to her. She knew nothing about vehicles other than they got her to where she was going. But the red part, that would be easy enough to spot.

"Do you hear me, Jennifer?"

"Yes, Mom." She let the curtains fall back into place. "But I don't understand your reasoning. Besides, I really wasn't calling to ask your permission. I was calling to let you know my plans in case you called this week and couldn't get in touch."

Dead silence met her ear from the other end.

Jenny rolled her eyes and let out a shaky breath. "Mom?"

Her father responded instead. "Now, Jennifer, look. Listen to your mother. You've met this boy one time and now you think you are in love. That's ridiculous. You need to stay in State College this week. Work on your classes. Besides, we don't even know these people."

"Two times, and we've exchanged hundreds of letters and talked on the phone every week."

"Two?"

Crap. She hadn't meant to let that out of the bag. "Ben and I met for the day back in August. No big deal."

Silence again. "Jennifer, when did you start lying to us? Is it that boy who is influencing you? Telling you to lie?"

That angered her. Ben was the sweetest, most kind and thoughtful young man she'd ever known. "Absolutely not. And if you got to know Ben, you would see that."

"I saw him the one time."

"Yes, you met Ben at the beach, but you barely gave him the time of day. The morning we left, remember? And you met his parents, too. You said they were nice people."

Her father didn't miss a beat. "We met them. We don't know them."

"Well, how am I supposed to get to know them if I don't visit?"

"It's not safe."

"It's Dickens! The Christmas village. How could it not be safe?"

"Jennifer. Don't push it."

"But Dad, please understand." She didn't, wouldn't beg. But she could feel the tears welling up in her eyes and she'd be damned if she'd let him hear her cry. She didn't want to defy her parents. Yet, they were forcing her hand. She was nineteen, and wasn't that old enough to make her own decisions?

"I've heard enough."

"Dad, the last thing I want to do is make you and mom mad, but this is not your decision."

Her father cleared his throat. "Jennifer. I am sending you to college to get an education. Not to go gallivanting all over the eastern seaboard meeting boys."

"Man!" she shouted back. "Ben is a young man, not a boy. An adult, and for that matter, so am I. I am not gallivanting. It's Ben and I am going. Oh, and for the record? I am not thrilled with the college plan, and you know that—college was your idea, not mine. So, excuse me if I am not as excited about it as you are, but we will discuss that another time. I have to go now, Dad. I'll talk to you when I get back."

"Jen—"

She hung up the phone and immediately felt panic well up inside her. Great. Now she'd royally ticked off her parents. That had not been her intent. She'd wanted them to like Ben and hadn't wanted to do anything to make him appear unfavorable in their eyes.

Had she screwed things up?

The phone rang again—she ignored it. Picking up her backpack, she glanced quickly out the window, saw the red pickup truck pull up to the curb, and headed for the door.

"Bye Claire. See you in a week!"

Ben's heart swelled the moment he saw Jenny running down the steps of the old dorm building. He shoved the truck into park, cut the engine and grabbed the keys, and threw open his door to run and meet her. Her infectious smile warmed his entire body as she flung herself into his arms. He caught her up and swept her around, holding her close.

She hugged him back so tight, then pulled back to gaze into his eyes. "Oh, Ben. You're here. I've missed you so. Did you come to rescue me from this horrid place?"

"Absolutely." Then he kissed her. Fully kissed her on the mouth, and then raining little kisses on her face like he needed her lips to breathe, to live. He probably did. Her mouth tasted like a sweet cherry lollipop—her lip gloss, he guessed. And the sensation sent him spiraling. Holding her close after all this time made his chest hurt, so full of love for her.

"Oh Jenny. I feel like I'm about to burst open inside. I am so happy to see you."

She looked up into his eyes and stroked his face with her fingertips. "I can't believe it's you, that we are finally together again. And we have a whole week! Oh, Ben. Let's get out of here."

He nodded. "I can't wait to get you home to see everyone, and to see Dickens."

She pulled back. "Are you tired? That was a long drive."

He shook his head. "No, I'm good. The trip didn't take me as long as I thought. About six hours. I started out yesterday after work and spent the night in a hotel off the interstate, about an hour away. I figure we have plenty of time to get to Dickens by late afternoon. Oh, there's so much I want to show you, and Mom can't wait for you to meet the rest of the family. She has all sorts of things planned."

"Oh, how sweet of her. But I don't even want to think about leaving you yet."

Ben's entire body trembled with happiness, but his heart ached at the same time. "Me either," he whispered, kissing her again. Then he grabbed her backpack and swung it over his shoulder. "Let's get going."

Jenny smiled and hooked her arm in his. "I am so ready. Let's get out of here!"

They chattered for an hour or so—Jenny more than him, but he didn't care. He loved hearing her sweet voice ring inside the cab of his truck and loved her sitting close beside him on the bench seat. He was beginning to think he always wanted her there, and that made his soul sing.

❄

During their ride, Jenny fell asleep, cuddled up against Ben's side. The sensation of being safe and happy had lulled her into a state of contentment, Ben's warm body next to hers. More time had passed than she had imagined as she blinked awake and heard Ben say, "Jenny, wake up, sweetheart. We are almost there. I want you to see this."

Stretching and sitting up, she looked out the wide windshield and saw a big sign on the right side of the road.

"Welcome to Dickens," she read. "New England's Christmas Village."

She turned to Ben. "We're here already?"

"You slept for a while."

"I'm sorry! I should have stayed away to keep you company!"

Ben's big smile captured her heart. "I was perfectly fine with you snuggled up against me." He pulled over and parked in front of the sign. "I think I might always want you next to me, Jenny."

"Oh, Ben. There is no place else I want to be."

Wrapping his arms around her, he nuzzled her cheek. "I love you, Jenny Anderson. I'm so happy to have you home with me."

"I love you back, Ben Matthews. It feels good here."

He gazed into her eyes, and Jenny knew she never wanted him to stop staring into them.

"Are you nervous?"

She nodded. "A little. I only met your parents briefly and I haven't met your sister, so I don't really know if they like me in your life. What if I mess up? What if I say something wrong?"

Ben laid a fingertip on her lips. "Sh. Not happening. They love you already. Everything will be fine."

"You're sure?"

"I'm positive."

Jenny relaxed a little. Maybe he was right. She'd trust his word. She just couldn't image how it would be if the opposite were happening—if Ben was coming to stay with her family for the week. She wasn't sure how her parents would deal with that.

Looking again to the Dickens sign, she felt better, though. "I am happy to be here," she mumbled.

Ben wrapped his arms tighter about her and nuzzled her neck. "Welcome to Dickens, Jenny. I hope you come to love it as much as I do."

"I already do," she said, and then kissed him.

FIVE

THE CHRISTMAS VILLAGE of Dickens

Ben's mom clasped her hands together and squealed as the front door to the Matthews' home swung open. Her expression was priceless, so inviting and full of cheer, and Jenny immediately knew she could come to love this woman. Mrs. Matthews reached for her son and waved him and Jenny inside.

"Come in here, you two! We've been waiting for hours. Oh my, Jenny. You look prettier than you did last summer. Fall agrees with you...which is good. Fall is sort of our thing around here."

"Unless it's Christmas." Mr. Matthews nudged by his wife. "Hello Jenny. Welcome to chaos, er, our humble abode. It's good to see you again." He leaned in and placed a peck on her cheek.

"Oh, thank you for having me, Mr. Matthews. I'm so happy to be here."

Ben's father grasped her hand. "Now, we'll have none of that Mr. and Mrs. Matthews stuff. We're family. I'm Calvin." He squeezed her hand.

"And I'm Maureen." Ben's mother leaned in for a hug too.

Jenny's lips stretched into a wide smile while being steered into the Matthews' home where they were greeted by not only Ben's parents but also his Uncle Herb—Calvin's brother, she learned—and Ben's older sister, Charlotte, and her husband, Brian. In fact, she smiled so big and so long, her mouth hurt.

But she didn't care. She was glad to be with Ben's family, and of course, with Ben—secretly relieved they were so welcoming.

Suddenly, her attention diverted when two young boys galloped in from the kitchen and halted in front of Jenny.

"Boys! Slow down." Charlotte sighed. "I'm sorry, Jenny. They are a train wreck."

Jenny took in Charlotte's harried expression, then crouched a little to make eye contact with the youngsters. The taller boy had an orange sugar cookie rim around his mouth, and the smaller one had chocolate smeared on his T-shirt. "Well, hello there, you two. So, which one of you is Liam and which is Logan?"

"You know our names?" The taller boy's eyes grew wide.

Nodding, Jenny said, "I do. Your Uncle Ben has told me all about you."

An alarmed look crossed the boy's face.

Ben stepped closer. "Yes, I told her everything."

"Everything?"

Leaning down, Ben whispered, "Yes, even about the farting incident."

"Uncle Ben!"

Jenny rolled her eyes and elbowed Ben. Looking at the

child, she said, "He told me no such thing. Now, I'm going to guess. You're Liam, right?"

"No." He pointed to the younger boy. "He's Liam. I'm Logan. I'm the oldest."

She stuck out her hand. "Well, of course. Hello, Logan. I'm Jenny. Happy to meet you."

He eyed her and tentatively touched her hand. "You, too." He paused for a couple of seconds, then added, "I'm six and in the first grade."

Jenny tilted her head. "Wow. That means you are really smart. I bet you are learning how to read already."

Logan nodded. "I read all the time!"

"That's outstanding, Logan." She put her hand up for a high-five and Logan slapped it, grinning.

Little Liam held up three fingers. "I'm three." Suddenly shy, he turned his face into his brother's side.

Jenny put out her fist. "Well, that deserves knuckles. Three is an awesome age." She pushed her fisted hand forward a little. Liam studied her, then laughed and gave her knuckles back.

Jenny stood, catching Charlotte's eye. "I imagine you have your hands full."

"I absolutely do, but I love every minute." Charlotte stepped forward and tucked her hand into Jenny's elbow, drawing her closer. "You have an easy way with children."

That surprised Jenny. "I do?"

"Yes. Seems natural."

"I've always liked younger kids. I worked in an after-school program in high school. Kids are fun."

"You'll make a good mom one day."

"You think so?"

Charlotte nodded. "I do."

Being a parent wasn't even on Jenny's radar. "Well, college first, and then maybe down the road..." But her mind wandered a bit, thinking about what it might be like to share parenthood with Ben. She glanced at him as he talked with his dad a few feet away.

"Well, of course." Changing the subject, Charlotte added, "Do you mind coming with me for a minute?"

Jenny noticed Ben, his father and uncle, and Brian heading toward the den. Ben tossed her a smile and a wink, and Jenny waved back.

She turned to Charlotte. "Of course. Ben appears occupied."

Charlotte rolled her eyes. "Get used to it. It's football day."

"Oh?"

"Didn't Ben warn you about that?"

"About football? No. But I'm familiar with football day."

Charlotte glanced at her watch. "It's nearly kick-off time. Once the game starts, there will be lots of yelling and cheering in the family room. Do you like football?"

Jenny stopped up short as they stepped into the kitchen and looked at Charlotte head-on. "I live in Pennsylvania and go to Penn State. What do you think?"

Charlotte grinned. "It's Boston College day, today. You, my dear, are going to have to pick a team if the Eagles play the Nitany Lions this year."

"Oh. Competition. I love it!" While Jenny's own family wasn't sports, she had always loved spending time with her friends at their homes on game days.

Charlotte grinned. "Good. I love you already. But first, we have a few things to take care of in the kitchen."

Jenny paused and gave Charlotte a semi-serious look. "Please don't tell me this is a 'men in the den, women in the kitchen' sort of thing. Is it?"

Charlotte's eyes rounded. "Oh, good Lord, no! Mom raises as much hell at the television screen as the men. She's more diehard football than any of them. And Brian knows his way around the kitchen better than I do. Smell those wings in the oven? He'll be coming in to check on them soon. Now, if it's hockey, though, that's a different story, and one we won't introduce you to this weekend."

"Hockey? Seems I need to do some homework."

"Just whisper the word and watch the guys' eyes glaze over."

A bubble of laughter tickled up Jenny's throat. "I think I love your family already."

"Well, that's a good thing." Charlotte took her arm again, and they moved on into the kitchen. "Because Ben sure loves you and that's enough for the rest of us." She slowed then and turned. "And I think you love him back just as much. Am I right?"

Charlotte's eyes darted back and forth as she studied her, waiting for a response. Jenny saw the concern and love there that Charlotte had for her brother. She laid a hand on Charlotte's. "I do, Charlotte."

Ben's sister placed her hand on top of Jenny's and squeezed. "I'm so glad."

Her throat about to close with emotion, Jenny continued. "I've never been in this much love with anyone," she said softly. "I know it's sort of whirlwind, and the distance thing isn't easy, but Charlotte, I love your brother so much. If you or your family worry that it's too soon, or that I would hurt him...."

Charlotte cut her off with a wave of her hand. "No. Not worried at all. Ben is a grown man, and we all trust his instincts. We love him and we love you too, Jenny."

The tension in her chest eased a little, and she exhaled a breath she hadn't realized she was holding.

"But enough of that." Charlotte slipped her hand into Jenny's and led her through the kitchen. "I actually need your expert advice for something. Ben tells me you are an artist and, well, I'm in charge of signage for the apple festival in a couple weeks. I have some ideas, but I'm not artsy. I need to get a design to the printer by Tuesday at the latest. I'm already past my deadline. Could you take a peek at my meager efforts?"

Jenny slowed her steps and turned toward Charlotte. "Me? You want me to give you art advice?"

She nodded. "Of course. Ben says he's seen your drawings and that you are fabulous."

"But I'm not sure I am the person to advise on this...."

Charlotte studied her, holding Jenny's gaze steady. "I value your opinion, Jenny. If Ben says you're good, it's good enough for me. Please?"

Jenny was momentarily taken aback. That Charlotte would take her art seriously was a bit overwhelming. Of course, Ben was always supportive—she'd sketch pictures and send them to him in her letters periodically—but Charlotte was practically a stranger. To have that kind of blind trust placed in her was not only refreshing but also a little intimidating. What if she gave the wrong advice?

"Please?" Charlotte tugged her forward. "All of my stuff is in Dad's office off the kitchen. Just a quick look?"

What can it hurt? Jenny squeezed Charlotte's hand and pushed her self-doubt aside. "Of course. I would love to. Lead the way!"

A rowdy cheer went up in the den, then Liam and Logan raced into the kitchen. Jenny glanced back as Ben's mom playfully slapped at their little hands as they scrambled up on bar stools at the island, grabbing for cookies. A timer went off on the oven and Brian burst into the kitchen, muttering something about his wings. Another cheer exploded in the den.

Jenny swiveled toward Charlotte.

"We better hurry. The festivities have begun."

Nodding, she followed Ben's sister into the office, her chest swelling with the fullness of family. For a split second, she thought of her own family back home in Philadelphia. Her sister would be in her room, in her own world, browsing through her magazines looking for apartment decorating ideas or makeup tips. Her dad would be watching CNN in the family room, perhaps with an Old Fashioned on the side table. Her mother would be meal planning in the kitchen, and then later grocery shopping for the week.

"Woo-wee! Run! Run! Run!"

"He's going all the way!"

"Touchdown!"

Jenny looked at Charlotte, while Ben and his dad shouted from the den. "Should we table this until after the game?"

"Exactly my thoughts."

The two women passed through the kitchen, grabbing food trays with sandwiches from Ben's mother on their way. Brian followed up with the wings. Jenny couldn't stop smiling. She loved this. All of it.

"Go Eagles!" she shouted, entering the room, and then setting the tray of sandwiches on the coffee table. She laughed when Ben grabbed her hand and tugged her down onto the sofa beside of him. She settled in next to him, feeling happily giddy. He grinned wide as he put his arm around her and squeezed.

On Wednesday, while Jenny worked in the hardware's backroom, sketching some ideas she had for Dickens Christmas Festival posters, Ben waited on customers out front. She could hear him chatting with the locals as they came in looking for such things as toilet plungers, or nails to fix the gutters on their hundred-year-old house, or screen-repair kits to keep the flies off the screened-in porch. Every need had a story, and Jenny smiled while listening.

Being with Ben at the hardware for the two previous days, she'd picked up the habits of the locals quickly.

Back in Philly, people ran in, plucked an item off a big-box store shelf, then hurried to check out and get home. She was as guilty of that as anyone. But here in Dickens, a trip to the hardware store was more of a linger. First, there was the declaration of what the customer needed, followed by the story about why they were looking for that item. Further amended by a related anecdote—perhaps the customer's cousin once had the same problem and said a *fill-in-the-blank* item would work. Did they have one of those?

More discussion ensued about the varieties of said item in stock, why this type was good for that, and the other one for something else. And so on. Finally, there was the official selection and purchase of the thing, a bit more conversation about random people and events or maybe the weather, and then the farewell and see you next time.

Whew! Just thinking about all that made her tired. But Ben —she was so proud of him—handled it all with ease and expertise. He had advice for everyone and a tool or gadget or solution to fix just about every dilemma. He was good at what he did.

The door slammed. Someone left. And another person entered. More chatter.

"Hello, Gabby. Did that chicken wire work for your pen?" Ben's voice rang out in the store. "What can I get you today?"

Gabby Harper, who lived one farm down from the Matthews' place, just outside of Dickens, Jenny had learned yesterday, needed supplies for her new baby goats—kid feed and formula and a couple of bottles, too, since one kid wasn't taking too well to her mama. Gabby worried she might not make it.

Yes, the hardware store stocked feed supplies for small animals, too.

Jenny listened to the conversation and smiled. She liked this town, the people, and she loved this place. The lifestyle was simple and the folks hardworking. It suited her laid-back approach to life and her artsy style—quite the opposite from the fast-paced lifestyle her parents maintained in Philly. Her dad was constantly on the go with his clients and court cases, and her mother flitted from one community project to another, while also teaching comparative literature courses part-time at Bryn Mawr. Candy had just graduated from Villanova and was circulating her resumes, while preparing to move out and get her own apartment.

The week so far had been pure bliss. On Monday evening she and Ben explored downtown Dickens after work, and he'd given her the grand tour of the Christmas shops. Tuesday, they headed out to the country, and he'd shown her the Christmas tree farm, the pond where everyone ice skated and played hockey, and then they'd hiked around Tamarack Lake. Each evening, his mother had fixed a lovely dinner and afterward, they'd settled in family-style in the den, and either watched television or just chatted.

She was so grateful for Ben's caring and understanding family. They had welcomed her with open arms. Already, she felt right at home. Every day, they made her feel wanted and accepted. No tension. No judgmental commentary. In fact, they valued her opinion about things, which was nice.

She found it all very refreshing.

Glancing about, she eyeballed her surroundings in the back room. While it was dusty and the shelves held decades of long forgotten items, she found beauty in the worn and aged wood beams, the paint-chipped shiplap walls, and the huge dust-streaked windows.

Laying her sketch aside, she went to the windows and looked out into the alley behind the hardware. The back of the building faced north. The light was diffused by buildings and trees but cast reflected light through the windows to brighten up the room—perfect for painting. Glancing back at the table where she'd been working, she noted the sunbeam highlighting her work, and had never felt happier or more fulfilled. She loved doing art, and this was, honestly, a perfect place to work.

She was grateful to Charlotte for giving her another project to work on this week. She'd loved her ideas for the apple festival, and now she'd moved on to Christmas. More than anything, she was happy to be helpful and contributing, and filled with a joy she hadn't felt for a while, happy that they valued her talent.

With a forefinger, she smudged the dust on the window, then glanced about for rags and cleaners. Finding none, she decided to ask Ben, and turned back into the room.

He stepped in, smiling, crossed the room and gathered her into his arms. "Finally, she left," he said. "I've been dying for a kiss."

His lips were soft and played over hers gently, then with more urgency. Jenny's arms went around Ben's neck, and she pulled him closer. The kiss deepened as their bodies aligned, and their hearts beat in tandem against each other's chests.

Jenny pulled back. "Whew. I think you missed me."

Grinning, Ben leaned in for a second taste of her mouth. "Definitely. I know I missed you. How's it going back here?" He glanced about. "Man, I should clean this place up."

"Oh no, it's perfect. I like the ambience. Except, I would like to clean the windows, if you don't mind, and dust a little. Perhaps rearrange a few things."

"Is that all?"

She smiled. "I think so. Do you mind?"

"Of course not. But you don't have to do it. Let me call someone."

"No. I don't mind. Honestly. I like working back here."

Ben eyed her. "In this dusty old storage room?"

She nodded. "Umhm. It has great potential."

"For..." Ben arched a brow.

"For creating. I like the old stuff. The beams. The soft, warm tones of the wood. The northern light filtering in... Just need to get those dirt streaks off the windows, tidy up a bit, get some supplies—with your permission, of course—and it will be perfect."

"Perfect? Supplies?" Ben continued to study her. "What are you thinking?" One corner of his mouth turned up into a grin.

Oh heck. Have I put my foot into it? I don't want him to assume that I am presuming I have a place here, yet....

Jenny opened her mouth to speak, closed it again, then finally said, "I'm just saying, Ben, that I enjoy being back here. For one, it's close to you. And when you are working, I might use this as a studio? To create, sketch, do projects for Charlotte, or whatever. You know, when I'm visiting."

Ben continued to smile and pulled her closer.

"Just when you are visiting?"

She cocked her head. "What do you mean?"

"What if you lived here? You know, with me."

Blinking, Jenny stepped back a little and looked at Ben. "Here? You mean, here in the hardware?"

He laughed. "No, silly. In Dickens. In my apartment upstairs. I mean, potentially, in the future. After some time has passed."

"Potentially?"

40

"In the future."

She glanced about. "With you?"

"Could you ever see yourself living in Dickens, Jenny?"

She studied Ben. What was *he* thinking? After a moment, she whispered. "Ben, I see myself here every day. I see myself with you, your family, the people. I see myself creating art back here in this room while you are selling nuts and bolts out front."

"Really?"

She nodded. "Yes, Ben. I hope you don't think I'm being presumptuous or rushing things, but...."

Ben stepped back. Jenny swallowed hard because she didn't know what he was doing or thinking. Oh, God, she'd said the wrong thing. She was talking about the future too much. About being here with him. And he wasn't ready, obviously, and it was just too soon. Now she was pushing him away.

"Ben, I'm sorry. It's too soon for that kind of talk. I know that. I...."

He put a finger to her lips. "Sh." Then, reaching into his pocket, he lowered to one knee and looked up at her. "I've been carrying this around in my pocket since I picked you up on Saturday, waiting for the most romantic moment I could find to give it to you. I almost did when we pulled over at the sign at the edge of town. I guess this is as romantic as I could hope for because I can't wait any longer." He popped the lip on a black ring box. "Jenny, I love you. Will you marry me? I mean, of course, I need to ask your father for your hand, and all that, but..."

A huge breath whooshed out of Jenny's mouth. "Ben! What?"

"Marry me. Please? I don't mean today, but one day. Of course, we'll need to wait until you finish college and I need to save some money for a house, but I don't want to wait to make the commitment to you. I love you, Jennifer Anderson. Marry me?"

Jenny went down on her knees too, eye level with him. "You don't think it's too soon to get engaged?"

"No, I don't. Not for me. I love you. I want to be with you forever."

"Oh, Ben... I love you too."

"Marry me?"

"But what about the distance?"

"We will find a way. We have so far. And it won't be forever. Now, what do you say?"

"Of course. Yes!"

Every tummy butterfly known to man—or woman—flitted through Jenny's gut as Ben pushed the engagement ring on the ring finger of her left hand. Her entire body erupted into some sort of dizzy happiness, and she couldn't stop the bubble of giggle gurgling upside while looking at the ring on her finger. "Oh, Ben, it's so beautiful."

The sunbeam pushed through the dusty windowpanes, glinting off the diamond.

Footsteps sounded through the hardware and a voice met their ears. The two scrambled to their feet, standing close together, holding hands.

"Ben? Jenny? Where are you two? I just stopped by to see how the Christmas poster designs are coming. Anybody here? Yoo-hoo?"

Charlotte burst through the storage room door, chattering away. "Ben? Jenny?" She halted at the door, gawked at the pair, and clasped a hand over her mouth. "Oh. My. God." She rushed forward, took a lingering look at Jenny's hand, then faced her brother. "Ben?"

Was Charlotte surprised or upset? Jenny wasn't certain.

Ben squared his shoulders. "Yes. You see right. I just asked

Jenny to marry me, Charlotte. And she said yes. Not right away, but when we're ready. In the meantime, we're engaged."

He glanced at Jenny and gave her a cockeyed smile, still holding her hand, and tugging her closer.

Charlotte's gaze passed between them. In one swift movement, she rushed forward and wrapped her arms around them both. "Oh my God. This is incredibly good news. I can't wait to tell Mom." Then she pulled back. "No wait. That's your story to tell, Ben. Yours and Jenny's. I promise I won't, but you must tell her soon because you know I can't keep secrets."

Ben chuckled. "We'll tell them at dinner tonight. I'm going to make reservations at Antonelli's. Can you come? Brian and the kids too."

"I wouldn't miss it. But I'll get a sitter for the boys. That place is too fancy for those monsters!"

Dismissing her brother, Charlotte turned to Jenny. "My goodness. I've always wanted a sister. Now I have one. Welcome to the family, Jenny." She embraced her with strong, quick hug. "I'm so glad it's you."

Slightly overwhelmed, Jenny didn't quite know what to say. Her heart simply ran over with happiness, and contentment.

She was engaged. To Ben. They were getting married.

A ntonelli's, an upscale Italian restaurant, sat on Tamarack Lake about fifteen minutes out of town as the crow flies from downtown Dickens. Ben reserved a table inside, since it was October, instead of on the deck. The scene looking out over the lake was spectacular with the beginnings of fall foliage.

Jenny sat with her hands in her lap, looking out the window. The dinner was yummy, Italian was her favorite, and she'd ordered the eggplant parmesan special. The company and conversation with Ben's family were equally lovely. She enjoyed being with them all very much.

Beneath the table, she nervously fiddled with the ring on her left hand—Ben put it there earlier and she wasn't taking it off—turning the diamond into her palm. She didn't want Ben's parents to see the ring until he was ready to tell them they were engaged.

In her heart of hearts, she felt she would be welcomed into the family. But honestly, she didn't know them that well and their reaction worried her a little. She could only imagine the look of shock on her own parents' faces when they would tell them, and the subsequent line of questioning and doubt. She sure hoped that was not the scenario they were facing with Ben's parents.

Quit going down that rabbit hole, Jenny. Ben's parents are nothing like yours.

Shifting a little in her seat, she nodded toward the window, changing the direction of her thoughts. "It's so beautiful here. This view looks like a picture in a magazine," Jenny commented. She glanced up as the server started clearing their table. "I don't believe I've ever seen anything so pretty in all my life."

Ben leaned closer. "Dickens is known for Christmas, but Fall brings a lot of tourists too, just to see the leaves."

"That's right," Charlotte added. "Oh, I wish you could come back for the apple festival in a couple of weeks, Jenny. It will be peak season then. You would just love it."

Again, she stared out over the lake. "I know I would. I wish I had my paint box. I would love to capture those colors out there right now. Even though it's evening, the light is near perfect."

Ben leaned into her shoulder. "Maybe you could come

back for a long weekend for the festival? I'd come get you. Remember to bring your paints."

She grinned and nudged him back. "I would love that, but we will have to see. It's such a long drive for you." She turned to Ben's family. "My father has a rule about me having my car at college—not in my freshman year. I understand, but it's inconvenient."

Charlotte interrupted. "Oh, my goodness." She gave her father a nod. "Doesn't that sound familiar, Daddy?"

Calvin chuckled. "I had the same rule for Charlotte."

"Except you caved over Christmas vacation my first year."

He nodded. "That I did. I decided if I wanted my daughter coming home to visit, she needed her wheels." His gaze lingered on Jenny. "Perhaps your father will come around."

"Maybe." She paused for a moment. "The thing is, really, I just want to make it through this semester. I'm not sure about going back to Penn State next semester. I'd like to explore other options. That's the hard conversation I need to have with my parents that I'm dreading—but in the end, I know it will be better for me."

Ben squeezed her hand under the table.

His father studied her, then leaned forward. "I'm not sure what the issue is with Penn State, Jenny, but whatever it is, stick out the semester and think it through. It's good to finish what you start, and you'll have a semester behind you. If pursuing other options is truly what you want to do, then perhaps have a solid plan for doing that to present to your parents."

Jenny smiled at Calvin Matthews. "That's good advice, and pretty much exactly what Ben suggested too." She glanced at her fiancé, suddenly feeling so glad that she had him in her life. "Ben has been very supportive, and I appreciate it." Then turning back to his father, she added, "My father wants me to go to law school, so I can become his partner in the firm after I pass the bar."

"And that's not what you want?"

"No. I want to open up an art studio. If I stay in college, I want to major in art."

Charlotte cleared her throat. "Jenny, you are so talented. Can you find a way to do that?"

"That's what I need to figure out. The thought of law school makes my stomach turn. It's just not me."

Ben put his arm around her, pulling her closer. "You know I want what you want, Jenny."

"I do know that."

"And we're supportive of that too," Maureen added. "Not that we are encouraging you to go against your parents' wishes. I'm not suggesting that. Just know that whatever you decide is best for you," she glanced at her son then, "and Ben, we support you, too."

Jenny had to wonder... Did they know already about the engagement?

She gave Ben's parents a smile. "Thank you. Everyone. But let's talk about that another time. I didn't mean to bring my current dilemma to the dinner table tonight."

"We're happy to help. Besides, you're family!" Charlotte grinned, then glanced off as if she'd said too much. "So, do you think you can come back for the apple festival, Jenny? We would have so much fun."

"I don't know if I can get away. I don't have another long weekend until Thanksgiving." She paused, searching Ben's eyes. "Which, by the way, I had hoped you would come that weekend to visit my parents with me." Turning back to his family, she added, "Could you spare him this Thanksgiving for a day or so?"

Maureen grinned. "Oh, we might suffer through it...."

"Under duress," added Calvin.

Ben chuckled. "Don't mind them. I would love to. And then I could—" But he cut off his words and glanced from Jenny to his mom and dad. "Actually, I'm really glad you all could come tonight."

Maureen shifted in her seat and fidgeted with her napkin on the table. "It was a lovely dinner, Benjamin. So unexpected and quite a surprise. Thank you for taking us all out."

He grinned. "My pleasure, Mom. You've been cooking all week, and I thought it would be nice to give you the night off."

His mother eyed him. "Well?"

His father smirked a little and glanced away.

Jenny wasn't sure what was going on. She glanced at Ben, who appeared to be tongue-tied.

"Well, Ben?"

"What, Mom?"

"Quit beating around the bush and get on with it. What do you want to tell us?"

Jenny watched Ben's gaze shoot to Charlotte, whose face immediately went *deer-in-the-headlights*. Then he looked at Jenny.

She nudged him under the table. Goodness. Had he changed his mind?

"Benjamin? Good Lord. When in the world are you going to tell us about that diamond ring on Jenny's left hand?"

A long breath whooshed out of Ben's mouth, and he grasped Jenny's right hand tighter. His palm was sweaty. Ben was nervous about telling his own parents. How would he handle telling hers?

"Mom. Dad," he began. "This afternoon... Well, I asked Jenny to marry me. Now, we know it's rather sudden, so we're not planning anything right away. She has some decisions to make, of course, as you heard. And I need to save money, and...."

Both Charlotte and Maureen burst up from their seats and ran around the table to Jenny, hands clapping, their faces beaming.

Maureen got to her first, hauling her out of her seat. "Jenny! Welcome to the family." Her arms went around her in a tight bear hug.

Charlotte bounced beside them, then dove in for a hug too. "I'm so happy for you and Ben," she whispered. "Oh, the ring!" She grappled for Jenny's left hand.

Jenny quickly twisted the ring back, and both women oohed and ahhed over the diamond.

"My goodness, but the young man has good taste," Maureen said.

"It's beautiful, Jenny."

"I love it."

Charlotte looked into her eyes. "You are perfect for him, you know."

Pulling back, Jenny studied the women. "I wasn't sure either of you were ready for another addition to the family, yet."

Maureen clasped both her hands around Jenny's. "Honey, I knew from the moment Ben introduced us to you and your family at the beach that you were the one. I couldn't be more pleased. And neither could Calvin."

She turned and reached for her husband. Chairs screeched as they pushed back, and the three men stood, shaking hands and patting Ben on the back.

The server came back with dessert menus. "Looks like a celebration," he said. "What can I get you for dessert?"

"Champagne all around." Ben's dad took the menus from the server. "And whatever else this crew wants. Bring the check to me." He looked at Ben. "My treat. It's not every day your son decides to get married." Turning to his family, he added. "Jenny, welcome. I'm so glad Ben found you."

Ben gripped Jenny's hand tighter. Turning, she looked into his eyes. "Me, too," she whispered. "Me, too."

SIX

NOVEMBER, Thanksgiving in Pennsylvania

J enny drummed her fingertips on the sofa end-table while staring out the living room window of her home in Philadelphia.

Please, Ben. Don't do this to me.

She'd caught a ride home from State College the night before with a high school friend she rarely saw anymore, but who also attended Penn State.

Giant dancing inflatables danced across the TV screen as the Macy's parade droned on in the background. Her mother twittered about in the kitchen with dinner preparations. That was her mother's thing—scurrying about appearing busy while she prepared, not cooked, the holiday meal. Mostly, she ordered the turkey already roasted from a local grocer and catered in the rest. The pies, she picked up at the bakery around the corner. Her order was generally in by mid-October to ensure she would not have to bake. Her preparations consisted of making a couple of family-favorite side-dishes—deviled eggs, a salad, green beans with almonds.

Every. Year. The same.

Jenny's father sat at his desk in his study, going over notes for a court case on the docket for Monday. He cleared his throat often, paced the room approximately every ten minutes, then returned to his desk to add some notations to his paperwork.

Candy was...somewhere. Probably fiddling with her new make-up or trying on the clothes she bought yesterday at the mall.

The older she got, Jenny felt she just didn't fit in with this family. Had she been adopted?

No. She'd seen the pictures of her mother pregnant. This was definitely her biological family. She guessed she was simply the oddball of the group.

Where *was* Ben? He was supposed to arrive mid-morning, and it was already pushing noon. The family meal wasn't until six o'clock that evening, so she wasn't worried about him missing that—but with every minute that ticked by, she grew increasingly anxious that something had happened during his drive, or that he'd chickened out.

But Ben wouldn't chicken out. Would he?

Her fingers halted their drumming.

No.

She knew him better than to think that. *He will be here, Jenny.*

Biting her lower lip, she resumed drumming.

They'd discussed this day, and how best to approach her parents—especially her father—to great end when she'd gone back to Dickens for the apple festival a couple of weeks ago. She'd hated for Ben to have to drive so far again, especially since she knew he was coming to Philly for Thanksgiving, but he had insisted.

Besides, she'd wanted to see him badly, missing him like crazy ever since she came back after the early October trip.

They'd had another fantastic long weekend together and neither of them had wanted to part. One of the best things about the weekend was that she and Ben were free to just be themselves, sharing their engagement news with his friends and others in town, without worry or concern. Everyone—Ben's friends and especially his family—had been so excited for them. She'd felt so good there, welcomed and happy.

Philadelphia just wasn't her happy place any longer. Her happy place was with Ben in Dickens—and always would be.

Another reason she was so antsy now, she supposed. That kind of support and excitement was likely not what would greet them this weekend, once her family heard the news. Still, she was so glad Ben was coming here to be with her. She needed him—needed his arms around her to make her feel safe and loved.

She needed his moral support as well.

There. A flash of red caught her eye down the tree-lined street. The familiar pickup truck pulled around the corner and slowed as it approached her home and angled into the driveway. A smile burst across her face so quickly she could feel it. She twisted on the sofa to watch him pull in and park behind her mother's Lexus. His truck looked ridiculously out of place in her upscale, manicured neighborhood—but not in her heart. That red pickup truck symbolized so many things to her. Love. Home. Ben.

It fit her, and that was all that mattered.

She flew off the sofa and headed toward the front door. Her father looked up from his desk as she passed his office.

"Jennifer, slow down. That boy has driven all this way. He can wait another minute or two. You don't have to fling yourself at him."

She halted. "That boy, Dad, is Ben. My boyfriend. Please be nice to him."

He arched a brow and stared. "I will be cordial."

"And make him feel at home, please?"

Her father lowered his pen to the desk. "Jennifer. This infatuation with this young man—you know it's not going to last. He's... Well, he's a small-town boy—I'm sure he and his family are nice—but they aren't our kind of people. You know that. Right?"

Jenny stared back. His words had taken her off guard, nearly cut her off at the knees. It took her a minute to respond. "No, I don't know that. What does "our kind of people" mean? I love him, Dad. You need to understand that. Ben and I are a couple, and we have plans."

"Plans?" He laughed. "Jennifer, it's puppy love. Please realize that for what it is." He picked up his pen and looked back to his paperwork. "Think about it."

She'd been dismissed.

"Well, excuse me while I go fling myself at my small-town, country, redneck boyfriend."

She glanced once more at her father—who didn't look up—then hurried toward the front door and yanked it open. Crossing the wide porch, she tripped down the steps, her stomach a jumble of nervous energy and disappointment with her father, and jogged across the lawn toward Ben, gathering speed all the way.

He was only half out of his truck when he caught her up in a bear hug embrace and planted a long, sloppy kiss on her lips. He threaded his fingers into her hair and held her face tight. "Oh, I missed you," he uttered between nibbles.

"Oh, Ben. Me too. I was so anxious. I thought you'd gotten cold feet!"

He pulled back, studying her. "Jenny, you know I would never do that."

She did know that. "I guess I just had to voice my fear. I know."

"We are going to get through this."

Nodding, she looked up. "You're confident all of this is going to work out. Aren't you?"

His head dipped. "One way or another, it will." He smiled.

Suddenly everything seemed all right. *One way or another.* Ben always made everything all right. Jenny leaned in and nuzzled his neck. "Um, you smell good."

"That's probably the apple cake mom sent."

"Oh!" Jenny placed her hands on either side of his face and kissed his lips. "No, it's you. Oh God, it's only been three weeks, but I've missed you so."

"Me, too, sweetheart."

"This distance thing is so hard—harder than I thought it would be."

Ben nodded, a serious look crossing his face. "I know, Jen. Maybe it will get easier. Or maybe it won't and...."

His pause gave Jenny a moment of concern. "Maybe what? Oh Ben, have you changed your mind about us?"

Ben cupped her face in his big hands. "Changed my mind? Never. I would marry you tomorrow. Today, if that were possible."

His gaze danced over hers, and she knew she would do the same. "I'd marry you this minute. I...." Her words trailed off, thinking about the conversation with her father.

"Are you okay?"

She nodded. "Yes. I just had a weird conversation with my dad. I'll tell you about it later."

He studied her face for a moment. "Okay. If you are sure."

"I'm fine."

Ben leaned in and placed another sweet kiss on her lips. He reached for her hand then, and she knew instinctively he was feeling for her ring. He'd done that often during apple weekend. She'd loved the way he fiddled with the engagement ring absentmindedly when they were holding hands. He pulled back. "Jenny?"

She exhaled. "I'll wear it after you've talked with Dad. I didn't want to take it off, but I knew they would see it if I didn't. My sister would make a huge scene. She expects to be the first one to get engaged and honestly, she's nowhere near that. I didn't want to tackle the subject of our engagement by myself." She clasped his hands. "I hope you understand. I need you beside me for this."

He gazed into her eyes. "I understand. So, do you think our plan is still a good one? To approach your father after dinner?"

"I'm not sure." She shrugged, hesitating. "I've been thinking—maybe too much. Let's gauge that by how the day goes. We may want to get through today and then discuss it all with them tomorrow."

"That gives us today to get comfortable with each other— me and your parents, I mean."

"Yes. I hope so."

Again, he studied her face. "Jenny, you're worried."

"I am a little," she admitted. "My family is not like yours, Ben. Your family, and everyone in Dickens, have opened their arms and let me in without hesitation. My family keeps people at arm's length until they get to know them."

"How do you get to know someone by keeping them at arm's length?"

"That's exactly the point...and the problem. My parents keep small circles and few friends. They are not hugely social beyond their work lives. And inviting new people into their small circle is very uncommon. I swear. Sometimes I think I was born into the wrong family." She laughed.

He chuckled. "Maybe. What about your plans for next semester? Have you brought that up yet?"

"No. I've been thinking that's also a discussion to approach tomorrow.... Or it may be one of those situations where I just know when the timing is right."

She bit her lip, glancing off. She'd decided about Penn State, had talked with her advisor at school, and now just needed to share the news with her parents. She was all set up for online coursework next semester, part-time. All she needed now was to get a job. She had some leads lined up.

"Well, there's your dad at the door. I suppose we should go in."

She glanced toward the house. "I guess so. Can you tell I'm procrastinating?"

"A bit."

Jenny glanced back to the house, then to Ben. "What can I help with?"

He pulled out the cake box. "Apple cake?"

"Got it." She gave Ben a smile.

His gaze skittered over hers for a moment, lingering, then he leaned in for a kiss. "It will be fine," he whispered. "I love you."

"I love you too, Ben. So very much."

Cake in her hands, she turned for the house. Ben followed, but after a couple of steps, stopped her with a touch to her arm. "Jenny?"

Turning, she studied him. "Yes?"

"I just want to say something."

"Okay?"

"I've been thinking and want to say this before we approach your parents with everything. There is going to be a lot coming at them, with your leaving school full-time and me asking to marry you. If things go south, if things get out of control, I want you to know that I am by your side, no matter what. I love you and we are going to be fine. Even if your parents aren't. Like I said, I'd marry you tomorrow, if you wanted. I want your parents' blessing, but I'm prepared to do whatever is best for us. I hope you are too."

Tears stung her eyes. "Oh, Ben. I'm about ready to ditch it all and run off with you tonight, and I wouldn't look back. But let's try to get through this, and then we'll see what kind of Plan B we need to come up with."

Ben nodded his agreement and hugged her tight.

"Jenny!" Her father's voice boomed from the porch.

She pulled back and whispered, "I love you so much. It will be fine." Then over her shoulder, she shouted, "Coming, Dad!"

They approached the house together, stopping as they reached the front porch steps. Jenny stole a glance at Ben, who looked up at her father, put his hand on the small of her back, and guided her up to the porch landing.

Ben sat his bag down on the porch, then extended his right hand. "Good morning, Mr. Anderson. It's nice to see you again. Thanks so much for having me."

Her father stared at Ben's outstretched hand and after several seconds, gave it a limp shake. Embarrassed was too mild a word to describe how Jenny felt at that moment. Angry was more like it. She knew her father, and she also knew what a weak handshake meant to him—disinterest. She'd heard him say it a million times. Now, he was obviously sending a message to Ben and to her. He didn't take her, or her relationship with Ben, seriously—and that made her doubt the wisdom of this weekend, entirely.

"No problem," her father said, eyeballing Ben. "Jennifer is

happy you are here." Then he turned and silently walked into the house.

Jenny heaved a massive sigh. Ben caught her eye and gave her an uncertain grin.

Plan B came quicker than he expected.

Thanksgiving dinner was nothing short of a disaster. Ben sat in the middle of it all at the Anderson's dining room table and immediately understood the depth of Jenny's dilemma. The family couldn't get through the salad without confrontation or judgement.

Mr. Anderson complained that the salad wasn't crisp enough. Did Mrs. Anderson make it fresh or buy it from the grocery?

Then, when carving the turkey, his commentary turned to the lack of attention to detail from the meat market. He was unhappy with the size of the bird. Why had she ordered a twenty-pound bird? She knew he didn't like leftovers.

Worse, Mrs. Anderson picked at Jenny. How long had it been since she'd had her nails done? She could use a visit to the hair salon—she'd make an appointment for her during Christmas break. And couldn't she have found something nicer to wear to dinner this evening? After all, it was a holiday.

Candy glanced at Jenny, tossing a smirk and rolling her eyes.

Jenny hid her embarrassment by lowering her gaze and looking down at herself.

Ben reached for her hand underneath the table and squeezed it.

"I think she looks beautiful," he said, studying her profile.

Jenny slowly turned his way, and he noticed the mist

gathering in her eyes. Her beautiful, bronze eyes. She latched onto his hand and whispered, "Thank you, Ben."

Candy rolled her eyes again. He still had to form an opinion of her, but at this moment, it wasn't super favorable.

Ben swung his gaze across the table to look at her parents, both of whom stared back with blank expressions and no words.

He thought about his own family back in Dickens. By now, they'd have settled in the den talking football or hockey, watching a game, or talking about an upcoming one. The atmosphere would be rowdy and energetic and fun.

Here, at Jenny's parents' home, he thought he might suffocate in the stuffy mood and the lack of kindness exhibited by her parents. He couldn't even fathom what an evening in the family room of this home might be like.

He sorely doubted they even gathered and wondered where they would all drift off to after dinner.

Mrs. Anderson spoke up then, turning the subject to her other daughter. "So, Candace, have you thought about furnishings for your new apartment? What style are you thinking? We could go shopping tomorrow if you like."

Candy sat up straighter in her stiff, straight-back chair, and smiled. "I've been looking at some lofts. Contemporary, for sure. With perhaps a touch of industrial for that upscale, urban look. What do you think, Jenny?"

Jenny cocked her head. "I think it could work. Maybe add a spot of Boho for interest. You know, splash of color here and there. Something unexpected."

Candy scrunched up her face. "No Boho. Definitely not. You're the artsy-fartsy girl. That's not me."

"It could be stunning."

"Everything is not an art project, Jenny. This will be my home."

"All the more reason to personalize it with things you love, rather than a carbon-copy of some picture you saw in a magazine. As I recall, you love those scarves you picked up in Mexico last year. Those would be lovely as decorative accents."

Candy stared. "They're scarves, not decorations."

"But—"

"No. Jenny. Thanks for the tip but I'm keeping with straight lines and monochromatic neutrals. It will be lovely."

"Of course. But you asked my opinion. I was just giving it." Jenny glanced at Ben and blew a thin breath through her lips, dismissing the subject.

He felt for her. Jenny was only trying to contribute, but once again, had been shot down.

"Whatever..." Candy waved her off. Obviously, she enjoyed being the shining star of the family.

Her parents doted on her, discussing her recent graduation from college and her pending job interviews. Mr. Anderson talked with her about where she should look for her apartment and that he would subsidize it for the first six months until she got on her feet.

The plan for Candy was to get a job with a law firm somewhere in the city—for experience, you know, and to step her foot into field. As her awareness and experience grew, she'd move over to her father's firm.

The conversation droned on between them for quite some time. Past the main course and into the pumpkin pie.

That same plan, he assumed, was what they expected of Jenny.

He glanced at her, sitting quietly to his right, and gently nudged her knee with his under the table. She peeked his way and moved her left hand to his thigh.

Was he wrong wanting to marry her so quickly? Should he hold back his feelings and let her explore the ideas her parents had about her future? But she really didn't want that future, did she? Or was she just saying that for his benefit?

Somewhere between pie and coffee, Jenny's father switched his focus. "So, Jennifer, let's talk about your class load. How are you doing?"

Her hand jerked. Ben noticed the startled look on Jenny's face and felt her sudden anguish in his heart. "Oh, fine, Dad. They are going fine."

Her father dropped his chin. "Just two more weeks and you'll be back home for Christmas break. Have you registered for next semester's coursework? Let's go over your schedule. I'd like to see you to step it up, take a few more hours now that this semester is under your belt. You can handle more. Let's move through those prerequisites. Thoughts?"

Jenny looked stunned, staring at her father, and then dropped her gaze to her plate. Her tongue ran over her lower lip. Ben could tell she was contemplating exactly what to say. He had the idea that she didn't confront her father often, and he wondered if she could do it now. Her fingers wrapped tighter around his fingers. Ben held on, hoping she realized he was on her side. Always.

"Jennifer?"

She looked up. "Yes. I have thoughts on that, Dad. I'm happy to talk to you about them, and I'd planned to do that tomorrow." She plunged ahead, the words spilling out of her mouth, as if she had to say them all now or forever hold them. "I suppose now is as good a time as any though.

"I've spoken with my advisor, and we've developed a new plan. I'm not going back to Penn State full time, I'm taking some distance classes, and I've switched my major."

"To?"

"Art, with a minor in business."

Jenny's father stood, tossing his napkin on the table. He

looked directly at Ben and pointed. "This is your fault. She never had these crazy notions until she met you."

"Dad, that's not true." Jenny let Ben's hand go and bolted up.

But Mr. Anderson's stare never left his. It bored into him. Ben was pretty sure he felt the depths of that stare deep in his gut.

"I want a word with you in my den. Now," he said to Ben.

He stalked away. The confrontation between him and Jenny was over in a flash. Ben watched him leave the dining room, swallowing the suddenly dry lump in his throat.

Fine.

He'd follow him to his den, and he'd take the brunt of his anger if it took the heat off Jenny. Any day of the week.

Glancing toward the love of his life, he took in Jenny's terrified expression. He stood, reached for her hand, and squeezed. "It will be fine," he told her. "I will be fine. And so will you."

Kissing her on the cheek, he left the table and followed the path her father had taken toward his den.

Jenny stood outside her father's closed office door. She'd lean in occasionally to see if she could hear anything more than the exchange of low voices. Every once in a while her father's voice would raise, and she heard his and Ben's muffled together, then nothing. Turning away, she'd pace the entryway from the front door back to the office door, and then in reverse.

She'd banned her mother and her sister from joining her as soon as Ben had left the table.

"Stay here," she said, looking at the two. "Clean up from dinner... And I'll clean up the mess with Daddy."

"You'd better come straight with him immediately, Jennifer," her mother had explained, "because you're walking on thin ice right now. I hope you know that."

"It's not fair to blame Ben. He had nothing to do with this."

"Your father won't see it that way."

"Well," Candy exclaimed, "at least I'm not the one in trouble."

"Oh, can it!" Jenny pushed away from the table and followed Ben. When she entered the entryway, the door to her father's office slammed.

She knocked.

"I'll deal with you in when I'm through here, Jennifer," her father barked.

She jiggled the door handle. Locked!

That's when the pacing began, her heart galloping inside her chest, keeping time with her steps. Her hand literally shook, so she clasped them together as she walked the room.

After a few minutes, the office door abruptly opened. Jenny spun toward it. "Ben!"

A sheepish Ben stepped into the entry and took a step toward her, then stopped. He took one look at her, shook his head slightly, then moved toward the door.

Her father followed him out of his office.

"Dad?"

"Get his bag, Jennifer. Ben is going home."

Anger now replaced the worry in her heart. She rushed toward her father. "No!"

She felt Ben's hand on her arm and turned his way.

"It's okay, Jenny. If you could grab my bag, I'll meet you at the truck. Everything is going to be fine." He winked, then reached for the front door.

Confused, she glanced from him to her father and back again to Ben.

"Then I'm going with him!"

"Go get his luggage, Jennifer. That's ridiculous. It's for the best. Ben and I agreed."

All she could do was stand there and shake her head. "Would someone tell me what is happening?"

"Later." Her father pushed past her and opened the door, ushering Ben out.

Ben glanced her way, then without a word, moved out onto the porch. Her father shut the door before she could watch him descend the steps.

Her mother stepped into the entry. "Here is his bag, Jennifer. Take it to him please, then help me clean up from dinner."

She whirled. "Wow. Are you serious? You're sending him on his way just like you're putting out the cat? Let him out and then help me the dishes? Does no one here have any empathy at all for Ben's feelings, or mine?"

She glanced at the small suitcase Ben had brought, sitting at her mother's feet now. Lifting her gaze, she panned the entry and her family, making brief eye contact with each. She moved forward and snatched up the bag. "*This* is what is ridiculous."

Her stare caught her father's as she headed for the front door. "You are wrong to make him leave. I'll never forgive you for this."

"I've done you a favor."

Her heart literally ached at those words. For a moment, she held his gaze, her head shaking. "You've broken my heart. I'm so disappointed in you." She turned toward her mother. "And you."

"Jennifer...."

"No, Mom. Don't do that. I'm not ten years old any longer.

I'm nineteen. I'm a grown woman. And I can make my decisions."

"Not when we are footing the bill for your college expenses." Her father's matter-of-fact demeanor broke through her hurt.

She swung back. "So, it's about money, then. Makes sense. Because you sure are not concerned about me as person."

"That's not true, Jennifer." Her mother stepped forward. "We love you."

"You both have an odd way of showing it."

She didn't wait around for any response. Tonight, she was done. With all of it. Picking up the bag, she yanked open the front door and rushed out onto the porch. She could see Ben waiting in the cab of his truck, the light on inside. When he saw her, he pushed his door open and met her half-way on the lawn, taking the bag.

"I want to leave here right now!" she told him. "Take me with you, Ben."

He put his arm around her and led her closer to the truck. "Let's talk about this."

"There is nothing to talk about. I can't live here anymore. I won't have them treating you like this."

He faced her. "Jenny, it's okay."

"No, it's not. Nothing is okay."

"It will be."

She studied his face. "What did he say? What did *you* say?"

Ben exhaled, pushing out a long breath. "I did most of the talking. He listened, sort of, but he already had his mind set. I asked him for your hand, to marry you."

"And?"

"And he flat out said no. That you weren't ready."

"And he thinks he can decide that?"

Ben clasped her hands. "Yes, he does. But Jenny, we know better."

Sighing, she held his hands tighter. "What do you mean?"

"We know we love each other. We will get through this."

"Really?"

He tipped his head toward hers, touching foreheads. "I love you. I asked him, he knows my intentions. I told him I would prefer to marry you with his permission, but if he couldn't see his way to grant that, then you and I would find another way."

"And what did he say to that?"

"That's when he stood, crossed the room, opened the door, and told me to leave. You heard the rest."

He put his arms around her and pulled her closer.

"I don't want to go back into that house."

He pulled back, cupping her face in his hands, peering into her eyes. "Go back inside. I'm leaving."

"Jennifer! Your mother needs you."

She gave the front porch a slight glance, noticing her father standing there, then looked back to Ben. "What are we going to do?"

"Listen to me, honey. Look. I'm going home. You're going to go back inside and mend some fences with your family. Smooth it over about your school plans and help them see that what you are doing is best for you. Focus on getting them to warm up to the new college plan."

"But what about us?"

"That's for us to decide, Jenny. I'm all for making our own plans moving forward. Is that okay with you? Take the weekend to smooth over things with your parents about school —it's important to me you get that taken care of—then go back to State College for the last two weeks of the semester as planned to finish out your classes. I'll call your dorm room

Sunday night at ten. We will make a plan from there over the next couple of weeks."

"You still want to marry me?"

He grinned. "More than ever."

"I love you, Ben Matthews. I want to be with you in Dickens."

He grinned. "Soon, sweetheart. Soon."

"Jennifer!"

She blew out a hard breath, nuzzling closer to Ben. "This was not how I pictured this weekend."

He kissed her nose. "Me, either. But in some ways, it's been good. Everything is out in the open. Now, we just need to deal with the fallout, smooth it over, and decide our next steps."

Jenny thought about that. "You're right." Tipping her head up, she touched her lips to his and burrowed her arms around his back, under his jacket. "I'm going to miss you. I can barely stand for you to leave."

"I always miss you, Jenny." He stepped back, glanced at the house, then focused solely on her. "I love you more than my life. I'll see you soon."

She nodded. "Soon, Ben. I love you too. Drive safe. Talk with you on Sunday."

SEVEN

SUNDAY, December 23, 1989, 11:46 p.m.

The Anderson's living room held a soft glow. The lamps were turned off, but tiny bulbs twinkled lights on the tree and electric candles lit up the windows.

Closing her eyes, Jenny inhaled deep, held her breath for a moment, then let it out slowly. After a moment, she blinked, spanned the room, and sat alone in the room on the overstuffed chair next to the fireplace. On the opposite side of the hearth stood their trusty Christmas tree. She was pretty sure they'd had the same one for at least fifteen years.

And there it still stood. Tall. Plastic. Silver balls. Red bows. And all that.

Boring.

Where did she get her creativity? It obviously didn't come from either of her parents. Had that bit of genetics skipped a generation or two?

She'd likely never know. Her father had been on the outs·

with most of his family for several years—she'd never really understood why.

"Maybe now I do," she whispered.

All the family gifts were under the tree. Her family had never been one to go overboard on decorations, or gifts. Her father's big thing was to put money into their savings account each Christmas—for their future, he'd always said. Her mother would stock her girls up on their favorite hair, makeup, and bath products. Then there was another gift from the two of them—something practical yet memorable, like a designer coat, or an expensive charm bracelet. There were also gifts from the girls to their parents, and to each other.

The room was pretty. The Christmas tone was obviously set. And she'd always loved how everything looked at Christmastime in her home. But this year, everything just looked—sterile.

Clinical. Empty.

Boring.

Sighing, she blew out another breath. This one was quicker, whistling through her pursed lips. She longed to be in Dickens. With Ben. Where she could smell the pine or cedar Christmas trees. Where whiffs of chocolate cocoa hung in the air and where homemade wreaths graced the front doors of most homes. Where kitchens were messy with flour and sugar while the cookies were baking. And where cinnamon candy and peppermint sticks tempted her with their sugary sweet-hot sting to her tongue.

Soon, Jenny. Soon.

Standing, she crossed the room to the tree, perused the packages there, and glanced to a side table where a basket full of Christmas cards sat. Her mother was still very traditional in her holidays, and she religiously sent out the cards annually. They received an equal amount in return.

Jenny thumbed through the cards. The Johnson's down the street sent one with a family photograph. Tom Doolin, from her dad's office, sent a one with a manger scene on the front. There was one from the bakery, where her mom shopped religiously during the holidays. One from the minister at their church. And on and on....

Reaching into her sweater pocket, she pulled out a homemade card—one she'd made earlier that day from construction paper, snips of wrapping paper, and some leftover ribbon. She'd used Sharpies to draw the Christmas scene and for the Christmas poem she'd written inside.

She opened the card once more to read the poem, then secured the piece of stationary on which she'd written a letter to her parents and tucked it inside. Without another thought, she put the card in the front of the stack in the basket.

Turning back to the tree, she crouched there and debated her next move. Earlier, she'd placed gifts under the tree for her family—one for Candy, a Boho pillow for her new apartment, and a joint gift for her parents, a framed picture she'd created from the beach artifacts she'd gathered last summer, and a sketch of their beach house.

There were three gifts under the tree with her name on it. One, was the basket full of personal products. It was too big and bulky for her to carry. One was from Candy, and the other from her parents. Both were small gifts and would fit into her backpack.

She took them.

D ear Mom and Dad,
      I know you both will be unhappy when reading this

letter, and I am sorry about that. I do hope in time you will come to understand the choices I've made, and why.

I am moving forward with my plans to go to art school next semester. I am taking distance courses for the time being. This feels right to me, and it is what I want to do. In time, I'll open a small studio and teach classes, or just create. I'll figure that out in the future.

I realize you want a more definite plan, Dad, but this works for me, and that's what I need right now.

While we have had a very nice few days since I've been back home from school, you know I am not happy since you forbid me to see Ben. I honestly don't want to choose between you and him, but you are forcing my hand. And choosing between you is not what I am doing. I am choosing, today, to be with Ben. But that doesn't mean that I'm cutting you out of my life.

I love you both, and Candy. You are my family.

I also love Ben. He and I want to be together, build a life together. Get married. We want to have a family one day. And we want to live in Dickens and raise our family there.

I want you to be part of that, too.

I know this is not your dream for me—but it is the dream I have for myself. I hope you can come to accept it in time. I want that and I hope you will.

In case you haven't realized yet, I'm not upstairs in my room. I left with Ben last night. We are heading to Dickens, and we plan to get married as soon as possible. Please wish us well.

I will see you soon. I promise.

Love, Jenny

p.s. Please spend the college fund on yourselves. Take that cruise?

p.p.s. I will call you when we get to Dickens.

❄

Ben turned onto Jenny's street. An uneasy feeling haunted his gut and had for the past few hours. He hoped that nervousness—or whatever it was—would go away once he arrived and saw her. Slowing the engine, he approached her house, watching the shadows of her lawn. As he pulled up, he turned off the headlights and sat idling for only a few seconds before he saw her.

She raced from the house and jerked open the passenger door of the cab.

His heart pounding inside his chest, he embraced her and exhaled so forcefully he felt lightheaded.

She squeezed him tight. "Oh Ben. You're here."

He pulled back and searched her face, noticing the tears there. "Ah honey. It's okay." He thumbed a few tears from her right eye. "It's all going to be okay."

"I know. Let's go."

He took a breath. "We will. There is one thing I need to do first." That lingering apprehension in his gut started up again.

Jenny looked panicked. "What is it? We need to go before they realize you are out here and that I am gone."

Staring into his beautiful Jenny's eyes, he sensed her panic. But he also knew he had to do what he had to do. He'd had a long drive to think it over and knew that part of the queasy sensation in his stomach came from the anticipation of what he had to do next. "Jenny, listen to me. I'm not leaving here until I talk with your father. It may be a quick conversation, but it's one I need to have."

"What are you talking about?" Her eyes darted.

He grasped her hands. "Jenny, look. I need to talk to him one more time. You stay here. Don't get out. Let me do this. I need to do this."

"Oh Ben, I don't know...."

"I do." He shifted and put his hand on the door handle next to him. "Stay here. I'll be right back."

She nodded but he wasn't certain she would stay put. He left the truck idling and headed up the driveway toward the porch. It was after midnight and he was certain Mr. Anderson would not be pleased waking up to someone on his doorstep, but he'd decided, and he had thought it through. It was the right thing to do.

He pressed the doorbell. Once. Then twice.

A light came on upstairs, casting a beam across the yard.

Footsteps.

Another light in the entry and then on the front porch. The door swung open.

"What in the world...." Mr. Anderson stood in his pajamas and robe, framed by the door casing.

"Mr. Anderson."

"It's after midnight, son. What are you doing here?"

Ben swallowed. "I've come for Jenny. I have asked her to marry me, sir. She said yes."

Jenny's father stared. "And what do you expect me to do with that information at his time of night?"

"I don't want to leave without you knowing my intentions. I have a judge lined up when we get to Dickens. We love each other and are getting married. I'd like yours and Mrs. Anderson's blessing."

His brow arched, and he laughed. Laughed! Obviously, he did not take him seriously.

"So, what are you going to do, kidnap her out of her bed?"

Mr. Anderson turned as his wife came rushing down the stairs. "Craig, Jenny is not in her room. She's gone."

Ben braced himself. "No. She's in my truck."

"Oh, Craig."

Ben saw tears in her eyes. It was the first time he'd seen any sort of empathy from the woman. The dreaded sensation in his stomach came back with full force.

Mr. Anderson pushed past him and stepped out onto the porch. "Jennifer!"

Ben backed up, stepping slightly in front of him and partially blocking his way. "I'd like your blessing, sir. I love your daughter and I will take good care of her."

"Hell no." He glared then, sticking his gaze onto Ben.

"I'd like to discuss this, if we could."

Blinking once, he studied Ben, then parked his hands on his hips and looked off toward the truck. "This is ridiculous. Fine. Just go and take her with you. If you two are hell-bent to get married, then don't let me stop you. I'm washing my hands of this entire situation. You'll learn your lesson. Stay in Dickens. But you'll never get my blessing, or my support."

Mrs. Anderson clutched at his arm. "Craig, please. Have them come in and let's talk about this together."

"No!" His gaze never wavered from Ben's. "Our daughter has made her choice."

Ben hedged a little closer to him. "Sir, if I may ask... I don't understand what you have against me. You've barely let me get to know you. I'm a good man."

Mr. Anderson stood and stared at him.

B en continued. "She loves you and her family. This shouldn't be a choice between me and all of you. She shouldn't have to choose. You are being unfair."

"Unfair! You roll in here in the middle of the night, lure my daughter out of her bed, are prepared to take her off to the woods in some god-forsaken village in the country, and I'm unfair?"

He squared his shoulders. "Yes, I believe you are being unfair."

"Then you are delusional."

Ben stepped in reverse. *I'm getting nowhere.* "Mr. Anderson, I have a good, reliable job. I'm a respected member of our community. My family has lived there for generations. When Jenny and I get married, I can support her and our future family just fine. We won't require any support from you, nor will we ask for it. All I ask is that you not alienate Jenny. She loves you and her family. She also loves me."

After a moment of staring, tit-for-tat, Ben turned on his heel and headed for the truck. *Seriously getting nowhere.* He'd thought he was doing the right thing and honestly, he was, but this scenario hadn't turned out as he had expected.

"Then go!"

"Craig, get back in the house." He heard Jenny's mother coaxing.

Ben made his way down the driveway. During the seconds it took him to walk to the truck, he tried to process the conversation with Jenny's father. Perhaps he needed a minute before telling Jenny anything.

He got in and slammed the door.

"Ben?"

Downshifting into drive, he stared straight ahead, and drove slowly down the street . "That didn't go quite as planned, but I did what I needed to do. It's done."

"Bad?"

"Let's talk about it later. I need to think."

"What did you do?"

He turned toward her. "I needed to ask for his blessing one more time. I had hoped he would have had time to think about things and reconsider. I was wrong. I'm sorry, Jenny."

"Oh, Ben. Are you okay?"

He nodded. "I will be. Let's get out of the city. Let me drive for a while and then I'll probably feel more like talking."

The look on her face made his stomach clench. He reached for her hand on the seat and slowed the truck a little. "It's okay, Jenny. I'm okay. Just come over here and sit close to me."

She scooted next to his side and cradled his hand in her lap. "Was he mean to you?"

"He was direct. But I expected that."

"Ben." Her lower lip quivered. "Do you still want to marry me?"

"Ah, hell." He braked, stopping the truck, and reached for her. Wrapping his arms around her, he held her close for a moment. "I can't wait to be your husband, Jenny Anderson. I love you so darn much."

She pulled back, looking into his face, smiling broadly. "I can't wait to be Jenny Mathews."

"Are you sure? No doubts? No cold feet?"

"Absolutely not."

He grinned. "I wasn't going to tell you until we got closer to Dickens, but I got in touch with the judge. She's able to marry us tonight if we want."

"Tonight? Wait." She glanced off, thinking. Her eyes flashed with excitement when she turned back. "It's after midnight, so that makes today Christmas Eve. We can get married on Christmas Eve?"

"Yes. I would like that. Would you?"

Jenny's eyes twinkled. "Oh, yes!"

The happiness Ben felt deep in his chest right then was practically overwhelming—not to mention the relief flooding his entire body. "Then let's get on our way. If we drive straight through to Dickens, we can be there early morning. That gives us time to rest up before we have to meet the judge."

Jenny leaned forward, kissing him on the lips. "Oh, Ben. Perfect. This is really happening, isn't it?"

"Oh, yes. It is." Looking down, he fiddled with the engagement ring on her finger. His voice lowered. "And I couldn't be happier, Jenny. You're making all my dreams come true."

She lifted his chin with her forefinger and stared into his eyes. "No, Ben. You're making my dreams come true. I can't wait for a lifetime of dreams together."

EIGHT

AT THE MATTHEWS' home in Dickens

"I think they got the weather wrong." Calvin Matthews turned away from the window and caught Ben's eye. That single statement put Ben on high alert. His father never joked about the weather.

"Who?"

"The people on the news."

"The meteorologists?"

"Yes. They're all saying the same thing, but I'm certain their forecasts are bogus."

Ben chuckled to himself, hearing his dad say a word like bogus. "How so, Dad?"

"We're going to get more than a skiff of snow today and tonight. For sure. As cliché as it sounds, I can feel it in my bones. Besides, I don't like the looks of that sky."

Ben and Jenny arrived in Dickens about eight o'clock that morning. Exhausted when they pulled into town, after having driven all night, they went straight to Ben's apartment over the hardware store. They slept through the morning and into the early afternoon. Eager to get on with the plans for the evening, they showered mid-afternoon and proceeded to Ben's parents' home for a short while before heading out to Judge Cameron's farm to get married.

His father's declaration of snow was not in Ben's plans.

"You think we are in for a storm?"

Calvin pursed his lips. A corner of his mouth drew up. "If I were to predict, I'd say we're in for a few inches, at the least. That dark blue-gray sky in the west worries me. The wind is picking up too. What exactly are your plans for tonight?"

Ben glanced to the corner of the den where his mother, Charlotte, and Jenny were chatting, oblivious to the conversation he was having with his dad. He lowered his voice. "The Judge says she can marry us at seven this evening. Then after that, we're heading to The Pitcher Inn in the Green Mountains. I got a room there after they had a cancellation. It was difficult finding something at this late date."

Calvin nodded. "I'm sure. That's a nice place. Does Jenny know?"

"Where we are staying? No. I wanted to keep that a surprise."

"Well, I'm a little worried about you driving up into the mountains with this storm coming in."

Ben was a little worried, too. He'd been watching the weather on the news, and the weather forecasters were not predicting anything severe—but his father was rarely off with the weather.

In the background, he heard the phone ring in the kitchen and watched his mom scurry off to answer it. "I'm trying not to worry, Dad. Maybe your bones are wrong?"

With a smirk, Calvin patted Ben's back. "My bones are never wrong, son."

But worry tugged at his gut. "I know."

His mother's head popped around the corner. "Ben? It's Grace Cameron. She wants to talk to you."

The uneasy feeling he'd had last night crept back. This might not be good. Had Jenny's parents somehow figured out who would marry them and try to circumvent the wedding? Surely not. Still, he hurried to the phone, eager to know what she wanted. "Yes? Judge Cameron?"

He caught Jenny's eye through the kitchen doorway as she stood and started toward him.

"I see. Yes. I understand."

He listened as Jenny approached.

"Of course. We will see you soon. Yes, Ma'am. I have all the paperwork."

The judge hung up, and Ben slipped the phone back into its cradle. Jenny reached for his hand. "Ben?"

"Let's step into the den."

"All right."

They did and faced his family. With a heavy sigh, he shared the news.

"That was Judge Cameron. She wants to move the ceremony up. Her son's flight was delayed because of weather, and she has to drive to Montpelier to pick him up tonight. She's afraid if we wait until later they'll get snowbound in the city for Christmas."

"Goodness," Jenny said, "is it supposed to snow that much? I haven't been paying attention."

Ben caught his father's eye. "I guess your bones are on track."

Calvin stepped up to the couple. "Grace is as good a weather predictor as they come. If the two of us are predicting a storm, then watch out. When can she do the ceremony?"

"Now." He turned to Jenny. "Is that okay with you?"

Jenny glanced around at his family, then landed on Ben. "Yes!" She bounced a little and gripped his hand tighter. "But I want to say something before we leave."

"Of course, Jenny," Maureen offered, stepping closer. "What is it? I've been concerned that something is bothering you, ever since you stepped in the door."

Ben watched Jenny take a breath, then draw her lower lip in with her teeth. Her gaze darting, she exhaled, and the words tumbled.

"I want to thank all of you for being so welcoming and open to me from the very beginning. I know Ben and I haven't known each other long—just a few months, actually—but you've trusted in me..." Glancing to Ben, she leaned in closer. "You've trusted us to know that we are making the right decision. This means the world to me. To us. I wish my parents could see what you see in us. That they were more supportive. They had plans for me. Unfortunately, their plans didn't mesh with mine.

"I want you to know, though, that they are good people. And Ben?" Her gaze fully encompassed his again, and he could see the mist of tears forming in her eyes. "I love him so much. He did everything right with my father. He asked for my hand in marriage, and even when my father refused, he went back and braved him again. I'm not sure that went too well either, but I love him for trying."

Ben felt his throat closing at her words. He'd not told Jenny everything about the conversation with her dad, and he needed to do that soon. Now, however, was not the time. "Ah, Jenny. I love you so much."

Maureen stepped closer to the pair. "I think your parents

will come around, eventually. I hope so, for your sake. And theirs. But as for us? We love Ben, and we love you too. I can't picture my son with anyone else. The two of you are perfect and I couldn't be happier."

"I'll second that." Calvin gave Jenny a hug.

Jenny beamed. "I love being part of this family!" She curled into Ben, and he wrapped his arms around her.

Charlotte rose, gave Jenny a squeeze and a smile, and then headed for the front door, talking all the way. "You know I love you, girl but I gotta run. If the old folks' bones are calling for snow, I need to get the boys from my in-laws, pick up milk and bread, and head home." She kissed Jenny on the cheek. Then to her brother, she added, "Love you, baby brother. Take care of her." She gave him a bear hug and stepped back.

"I will." Ben smiled at his sister and watched her leave. Turning to Jenny, he added, "Well, I guess that's our cue. Ready to get married, Jenny Anderson?"

"More than ready." The look on her face then, as her eyes glazed over with love, warmed his heart and soul. *Let it snow. I have everything I need right here.*

J enny pushed one arm into her coat and felt a sudden flash of panic. She stopped up short and turned toward Ben. "Oh, no."

Ben finished shrugging into his coat. "What is it?"

"I forgot to call my parents. I was so tired this morning and then got caught up in everything this afternoon. Do I have time to give them a quick call before we meet the judge?" An edgy sensation rippled through her stomach and she placed a hand on her abdomen.

"Of course, we do." Ben's gaze dropped to her hand. "Are you okay?"

"I'm fine." She smiled then, nervously. "May I call from here? I can pay your parents back for the long-distance call."

"You'll do no such thing." Ben's father stepped up behind them. "Calling them is an excellent idea. Come into my office, Jenny. You'll have more privacy there."

"Oh, thank you. That would be great."

Her stomach muscles grew taut under her hand. She'd been happy and excited a few minutes earlier, and now she was a jittery wreck. What exactly would she say to them?

The truth. Just tell them the truth, Jenny.

Ben's dad smiled, and she found comfort in his gentle, caring ways. She followed his lead as they headed into his office. Ben held back until she reached for his hand and tugged him along.

"Do you want to do this alone?"

Her gaze played over Ben's face. "No. I want you with me if you don't mind."

He gave a quick nod. "Then I'm there. Always."

Calvin ushered them inside, then slipped out the door, softly closing it behind him. Jenny looked at Ben. "I guess it's now or never."

"Jenny, before you call, I want you to know something."

She studied his face, listening. "What is it, Ben?"

"You were right earlier. I tried to smooth things over with your dad, and it didn't go well."

"I assumed that Ben. But what aren't you telling me?"

"I'll just say... Well, your father wasn't very pleased with our plan."

"Did he get angry?"

"He was extremely direct. I wonder... He may not be receptive to your call."

That sounded exactly like her dad. He was an extremely direct person. The lawyer in him, she assumed. "What did he say?"

Ben hesitated.

Jenny sensed he didn't want to have this conversation right now. "Ben?"

"It will take a good twenty minutes to get to the judge's farm," he told her. "We'll talk more about what happened last night on the way there, or maybe it can wait until tomorrow. Right now, I think you should get this call over with, so you can let it go for a while. After all, we have a wedding to get to."

Jenny instantly felt better. Somewhat. "Yes, we do." She angled her head slightly to give him a quick kiss on the lips. "You're right." She moved closer to the desk and picked up the phone receiver. After a brief pause and a deep breath, she dialed the number.

And waited.

On the fourth ring, her mother answered. "Hello?"

"Mom?"

"Oh, my goodness. Jenny? Where are you?"

"Mom, you know where I am. Didn't you read my note?"

"Yes. Yes, of course I did. So, you're in Dickens? Are you married? You know I had hoped that we could have a big wedding. Do all the mother-daughter things that happen when a young woman gets married. Instead, you're.... Eloping." She said the last word with dread in her voice.

Her mother choked up a little and stopped talking.

Jenny's stomach sickened at her mother's lengthy sigh.

"Mom, it's okay. Let's do some mother-daughter wedding things later. Like a shower or something."

"Could we?"

"Of course, we can."

"But are you married yet? If not, maybe you could hold off?"

"Mom, no. We are getting married tonight. Within the hour."

There was another long pause on the other end. Then, her mother said, "Well, if you are sure."

"I am." Jenny hesitated before asking the next question. "Mom? Where is dad?"

Again, another deep sigh from her mother. "He's in the den. I think, maybe, you shouldn't talk to him tonight."

"Why? Mom, what's going on?"

Silence.

"Mom?"

"Jenny, he is not taking this well."

"If he hadn't been so darned stubborn and would only listen, then perhaps he wouldn't be so upset. But you know daddy...."

"You know he doesn't accept change well."

"Mom, he—"

She heard some shuffling from the other end. "Wait. Craig? I'm talking...."

"Mom?"

Another gap in the conversation. Then, her father's voice came through more loudly than her mother's. "Jennifer?"

"Dad?"

"I didn't expect to hear from you."

"But I said in my note I would call. Did you read the note?"

"Your mother said something about that."

"But you didn't read it."

"No. I have no need to read it."

That pained Jenny a little. "But she told you I was going to call. Why wouldn't you think I would?"

"Because you made your choice, Jennifer. You have a new family now."

"Oh, good gracious."

Her stomach muscles clenched, and the queasiness escalated. Lights danced inside her head. Good Lord, she could not pass out... "Dad, I do have another family now. But I also have my own family and I love you all. This is not an either-or situation. I get to keep you both."

"Well, that's debatable."

"What do you mean by that?" Pacing away from the desk, she glanced at Ben, and pushed away the hurt of those words.

"Think about it."

"Dad? I don't understand." She felt abruptly abandoned. Like her parents had dropped her off at school and didn't come back to pick her up at the end of the day. What was going on here?

"I'm hanging up now, Jennifer. Look. Don't call back. It only upsets your mother. You've made your choice, now live with it. As I told Ben last night, I've washed my hands of this entire situation. You're on your own. There is no need for you to call back or come back here ever again."

The other end of the line fell silent. A few seconds slogged on, followed by a deep sigh. Then Jenny heard the phone click off.

"What? Wait. Dad?" She turned, catching Ben's eye, and slowly, quietly set the phone back into the cradle. She didn't want to cry, but knew tears were close.

I can't walk out of this office crying... Not on the way to my wedding? How would that look?

"Jenny? Are you okay?"

She nodded. Her chin jutted up. "I'm fine. Let's go." She sniffed.

"How did it go?"

"I don't want to talk about it right now. Maybe tomorrow. We have a wedding to get to." She realized she was echoing his words from earlier, but honestly, her head was swirling right now, and she didn't know what to think. Squaring her shoulders, she turned and grasped the office doorknob and twisted it. She had to get out of this small room—her palms were sweating and her cheeks hot—and then figure out how to quell the conflicting emotions battling inside her heart and her head.

"You're sure?"

She whirled back. "Yes. I'm sure. Don't bug me right now. Okay? I need to process that call, just like you had to process things last night. Which obviously you didn't do very well because evidently, there were some things said then that you have chosen not to tell me. How could you do that?"

"Jenny, let me explain."

She waved him off. "No. There is no time."

Ben glanced at his watch and nodded his head. "You're right. We need to go."

"Yes. I want to leave. The judge is waiting."

This was not how he had pictured the drive to his wedding.

Ben squinted at the windshield, trying to see the road ahead. The snow squall had erupted over them about five minutes away from his parents' house. Having slowed the truck significantly, he crept along, trying to keep the vehicle on the right side of the narrow country road, while simultaneously glancing at Jenny to make sure she was all right.

She'd not said a word since leaving the house.

All he'd seen of her since getting into the truck was the

87

back of her head—she seemed determined not to look at him and to stare out the window.

This is ridiculous.

He needed to talk with her and wasn't sure which subject to broach first. Was it safest to first tackle what happened in his dad's office? Or should he attempt to suggest that the snowstorm had likely waylaid their wedding plans?

Neither subject was pleasant. He could be playing whack-a-mole for all he knew. Nevertheless, he had to say something. The quiet in the truck cab was driving him bonkers.

"Jenny, sweetheart... I'm sorry I didn't tell you what your dad said. Okay, maybe I should have, but I thought I was protecting you." Nothing like hitting the nail, er, mole straight on the head.

"You had no right *not* to tell me." Finally, she spun around to look at him, her eyes flashing, and her hair whirling around her forehead like cotton candy caught up in a swirl of static electricity. "He doesn't want me to ever come home again? I needed to know that."

"I should have told you. You're right."

"What did he say exactly?"

Ben cleared his throat and plowed ahead. "He said he was washing his hands of the situation. For us to go on and get married, but that he would never give us his blessing or his support."

Jenny's eyes grew wide, then slowly, she rotated to stare out the windshield. "We were dismissed."

"What?"

"It's what he does. Once he washes his hands of something, or someone, it's over. I've seen him do it with clients, his brother, and a few friends. He pushes them away and never has contact with them again. Remember what I told you? He keeps the circle small. And he just cut me, rather us, out of his life. I am honestly shocked. I never thought he would do that to me."

"Oh, Jenny." Ben's heart was about to burst for her. He reached for her hand.

She pulled it back and shoved it into her coat pocket.

Well. That certainly isn't good. He tried to ignore the fact that he, himself, suddenly felt dismissed. Change the subject?

"This storm is getting worse."

Jenny's right leg started jumping up and down—nervous, he guessed—her foot tapping on the floorboard. "How much longer until we reach the judge's farm?"

"Jenny, to be honest, I've totally lost any sense of where we are in this whiteout. I can't see a darned thing but snow and I'm getting a little concerned about trying to find her farm in this weather. The lane back to her house is narrow and unpaved, and she lives at the top of a steep hill."

"Are you saying we need to turn back?"

"I'm saying I don't know if I can go on. Or back. I need to find a pull-off."

"Then what?"

"We'll cross that bridge when we get to it."

"Ben? I'm serious. Are we in trouble here?"

He slowed the truck and looked her way. Her eyebrows were knit in worry and her eyes still held the mist of tears. "Jenny, I don't know. Maybe."

"Great. That's all we need."

Ben sighed. "Look. Maybe we should try to do this another time. This weather is a bear. Besides, I'm not sure either of us are in the right frame of mind to get married today."

She jerked closer to him on the bench seat, full tears in her eyes now. "And I'm not sure why you didn't tell me last night that my father practically disowned me. Were you afraid his tactics would work on me and that I wouldn't come with you?"

"That never entered my mind, Jenny. I never doubted that you would come with me."

"Well, I'm doubting right now that we ever will get married."

Ben braked hard. The rear of the truck skidded to the right. He stared at Jenny. "What does that mean?"

She didn't hesitate. "It means I'm not sure we should even get married, Ben. Let's just forget it for now. There is too much going on in my head, and there is the snow, and I need to talk with my mother because she sounded upset on the phone."

He edged closer to her. "Jenny, you're right. There is a lot going on. It's not the time to decide about getting married, or not. It will happen. Just not tonight, I fear."

She shook her head. "We can't get married until I figure out this thing with my family."

Nodding, he couldn't disagree with that. "All right. That's fair. I know we can't get married tonight, given the situation, and I'll give you time to figure out the family dynamics... But Jenny Anderson, I don't want to wait forever for you to be my wife."

The look she gave him sent his stomach into a downward spiral. Her eyes were narrow, her gaze determined. "Ben, I don't know when I will be ready. It wouldn't be fair to you, or to me, to put a timeframe on this right now."

A timeframe?

Twenty-four hours earlier, she couldn't wait to get out of her parents' house. Now...?

"So, our marriage is off the table?"

Her eyes widened. "Yes. For now. I don't know if I can marry someone who keeps things from me. I need you to always be up front with me, Ben. You didn't tell me what my father said, on purpose."

"And I explained that!"

Ben pushed back and leaned against the drivers' side door, staring out at the road ahead of the vehicle. The truck was idling, the wipers pushing wet snow to the sides. He couldn't stay here, parked in the road. That could be a recipe for disaster should someone come up behind him on the highway.

Down the road, between the swipes of windshield wipers, he spotted a mailbox to the right. That gave him a clue to where they might be. They needed off this road. If there was a mailbox, then there was a lane to the right. Or should be.

There. Shifting into drive, he eased the truck forward, then after several feet, pulled off and parked the truck in the entrance, but kept the engine running. Wet snow pelted the roof and the windshield. He turned to Jenny.

"Look. Let's put the marriage discussion aside for a minute. I didn't tell you what your dad said because I didn't want to hurt you."

"Seriously, Ben? Not telling me *did* hurt me. Can you imagine how I felt when I heard my dad say those words?"

"What did he say? I could only hear one side of the conversation. Yours."

"He said basically what you said. He was washing his hands of the situation. That I was on my own and that I shouldn't call or come back home, ever again. He basically kicked me out of the family and suddenly, I feel so lost. I don't know what to do."

"Oh hell. Come here, Jenny."

Ben gathered her close and wrapped his arms around her, tight. "It's okay, sweetheart. We are going to work this out."

"We really aren't getting married. Are we?" She raised her head and searched his eyes.

"Not tonight."

"Ben, I'm having serious doubts. Second thoughts. I'm sorry. I'm a little confused and upset. I guess I'm a mess."

He figured as much. While the thought of that pained him to the core, he had to keep faith in their relationship that it would work out. "It's okay, Jenny. We will work through this. But right now, my major concern is keeping us safe. I'm not sure we can get out of this driveway."

"What are we going to do?"

Ben stared ahead, out the windshield. The wipers were working overtime shoving the wet snow off the glass. Occasionally, when he got a peek ahead of them in the distance, he thought he could see a light. If he was where he thought he was, this could be the old Holly Hill farm, and hopefully the Peterson's, an older couple who owned the farm, were home tonight.

"We're going to walk."

"In this weather?"

"It shouldn't be far. We really don't have a choice. If we stay here, the snow will pile up. We'll run out of gas and besides, it's dangerous to run the engine if the snow is piling up around the car."

"Carbon monoxide."

"Yes."

"We need to get someplace."

"Yes." He nodded. "I see a light up ahead, off and on, through the snow. We're going to layer up and head toward it before the power goes out and we can't find it again."

"Oh Ben. I'm a little scared."

He hugged her again. "We are going to be fine. I won't let anything happen to you."

Or us.

NINE

HOLLY HILL FARM, Christmas Eve

Near tears and exhausted from trudging through the quickly accumulating snow, Jenny stumbled up the porch steps of a rather large farmhouse—what she could see of it anyway—while eyeballing the light to the right of the front door. They'd used that porch light as their beacon, all the while praying that someone was home. Her cheeks felt frigid, and she feared if the tears in her eyes fell, they would freeze right to her face.

That would be awkward, not to mention ugly.

She had no clue how far they had walked. It could have taken them ten minutes to get this far, or an hour—she literally had no sense of time, distance, or direction. She simply followed Ben in the swirling snow as he tugged her along, his arm securely linked with hers to keep her on the right track and moving forward.

Ben stomped his feet on the wooden porch as they

approached the door. Not as much snow had accumulated in that area. He rapped on the storm door and waited. After a moment with no answer, he glanced at Jenny, and then tugged on the outer door handle. It fell open with two jerks.

He knocked again, harder, on the inside wooden door.

A faint, female voice came through from the other side. "Who is out there?"

"Mrs. Peterson? Is that you? It's Ben Matthews. My truck's stuck in your driveway. May we come in?"

The door creaked open slightly, about an inch, and Jenny could see an older woman hesitantly peeking out in the space between door and frame. "Ben? My stars. Get in here." She opened the door wider, noticed Jenny standing there too, and waved them both inside. "You poor girl. You, too!"

"Oh, thank you," Jenny breathed. "We are so cold."

Mrs. Peterson fluttered about in her bathrobe and nightgown, fuzzy bedroom slippers on her feet. Her white hair was caught up in a clip, with tendrils of curls spilling out around her neck. "Get those wet things off, you two. Shoes first. Ben, put them over by the fire. Give me your jackets."

"Oh no," Ben responded. "We'll get you all wet. Just tell me where to put them and I'll take care of them."

They stood in the entryway, while the older woman tottered off toward the dining room, chattering all the while under her breath. Jenny glanced at Ben then followed her as she grabbed a straight-back chair. She suspected Mrs. Peterson was close to eighty years old, but she wrangled the two dining chairs with ease.

"Here," she said to Jenny. "Let's drag a couple of these over into the living room by the stove and we'll hang your wet things on them. It will be fine. These old chairs have seen more wet coats than I could likely count."

Shrugging out of her coat, Jenny thanked her, and grasped

the top of a chair. "I don't know what we would have done if you'd not been home." She crossed the entry with her chair and placed it in front of the stove. Turning, she went back to help Mrs. Peterson. "I don't mind admitting I was a little scared. Thanks again, so much, for letting us come inside."

The woman beamed. "Oh, pish. It's what we do. Isn't it? Help each other out in times of need?" She scooted her chair across the plank floor, then glanced toward the stove. Jenny took the chair the rest of the way. Mrs. Peterson pointed to Ben. "There. That's good. Not too close now, we don't want those coats to spontaneously combust!" She laughed.

"Oh my. Would they?" Jenny asked.

Mrs. Peterson shrugged. "I have no clue, but it sounded good, didn't it?"

It was Jenny's turn to laugh.

"So, Ben, is this your new girlfriend? I heard in town that you had one. Been sneaking off to Pennsylvania, I understand, just to see her."

Jenny glanced at Ben, who slowing turned away from the stove to face them. "Yes, Mrs. Peterson. I'm sorry I didn't introduce you when we came in the door. This is Jenny Anderson. She is my..." Ben paused, looking at Jenny. She could almost read the question darting across this face. *What am I to him now? Fiancée? Girlfriend?*

"Fiancée," Jenny said. She gave Ben a warm smile, then looked at Mrs. Peterson and fluttered the fingers on her left hand. "See? Ben proposed and gave me this beautiful engagement ring." It was all true, of course. Ben had proposed and given her a ring, and she was technically still his fiancée. The fact that they'd argued and talked of postponing the wedding didn't enter into this equation.

Did it?

We really aren't getting married. Are we?

Not tonight.

Ben, I'm having serious doubts. Second thoughts. I'm sorry. I'm a little confused and upset.

Mrs. Peterson drifted toward her. The action jerked Jenny out of her thoughts.

"Oh my. What a beautiful ring. What a lucky girl you are." She paused, looking into Jenny's eyes.

Lucky? She supposed she was. Then why was she so confused?

Mrs. Peterson continued. "The ring is lovely, Jenny, but I didn't mean you were lucky because of a silly diamond." She looked at Ben then and Jenny followed her gaze. "Ben Matthews is one right fine young man. None better. And so's his family. You're lucky to call them your own."

And she knew she was. She just hoped she could still call them her own, in time. Once she'd worked things out. Jenny's gaze drifted to catch Ben's, and he held her captive for a moment with his stare.

"Well, I need to go check on Harold," Mrs. Peterson said, then glanced at Ben. "He's not well, you know. His oxygen and all that. Lungs are just giving out. I need to make sure he's okay."

Ben took a step. "Is there anything I can do to help you?"

At that moment, the lights in the room flashed brighter, then dimmed, flashed once more, then went completely out.

"As a matter of fact," Mrs. Peterson called out in the dark. "There is. The generator is on the back porch. Gas can too. We need to get that thing started up so Harold's oxygen machine will run. We have a few tanks, but they won't last for long. Now, I need to tend to him."

"Will do," said Ben.

"Mrs. Peterson!" Jenny called out. "Wait. I'll go with you and help."

The woman reached for her, and Jenny took her small, soft hand. "Let's take it easy. We don't want to trip over anything."

"You are a dear. Just as nice as Ben. I'm sure you're going to make a fine couple." She patted her hand then and added, "Please help me get to my husband. He needs me."

I'm sure you're going to make a fine couple.

Ben pushed his arms into his wet coat by the light of an outside security pole light shining in the window, that somehow was not affected by the power outage. He glanced about the living room for a flashlight or lantern. Finding none, he slowly made his way down the hall in the same direction as the women and called out softly.

"Mrs. Peterson? Do you have a flashlight or two?"

The voice came from just inside a room around the corner. "I have one here," she told him. "But look in the kitchen, in the pantry to the right of the stove. There should be another one, and a couple of those battery-powered lanterns. Could you grab those too?"

"Of course."

He found everything, all the while his brain working over Mrs. Peterson's words about them being a *fine couple*, and Jenny's admission of her being his fiancée. Did she say that just to make things easier for him, or did she really intend to stay his fiancée? Earlier in the evening, he wasn't sure what the state of their relationship was.

Approaching the bedroom door, he saw the soft glow of the flashlight a few feet away. "Here are the lanterns," he said quietly, not wanting to wake Harold.

Jenny tiptoed his way, the flashlight bobbing in the dark as she grew closer. "Thanks, Ben," she whispered.

The soft light cast a warm glow over Jenny's face and for a moment, his heart clutched from loving her so much. She was so pretty standing there, looking up at him. Her big eyes held an expression he wasn't sure he could put his finger on, yet somehow, he felt everything was going to be okay. Eventually.

"Let me turn one on for you," he said, then fiddled with a switch on the bottom of the lantern to turn it on. More light flooded the area around them.

"Thanks, Ben."

He grinned. "You're welcome."

"I'm going to take this over by the bed now, so Mrs. Peterson can see her husband."

"Of course. Right."

Her eyes were still big and round and drawing him in, much like they did that day at the beach. But he stepped back. He was pretty sure the attraction was all from his perspective. He still had no clue how Jenny felt about the entire situation.

"I should get that generator going."

Nodding, Jenny stepped back as well. "Be careful, Ben. Please?" Worry crossed her face then and flooded her eyes.

"Always."

He turned and headed toward the door.

Jenny carried the lit lantern closer to where Mrs. Peterson sat beside the bed. The woman fiddled with an oxygen tank and tubes, and some sort of device that sat atop the tank where you turned the oxygen off and on. Mr. Peterson needed the tanks to replace the machine that wasn't working now due to the power outage.

Jenny placed the lit lantern on the floor, handed the flashlight to Mrs. Peterson, and found the switch on the second lantern to light it as well. "I'll set this one on this table over here," she told her.

"Yes, please," she replied. "Then, can you help me move another couple of tanks closer to the bed? They are over there by the closet. I need to see how many we have to estimate how many hours of oxygen we have here."

Those words panicked Jenny a little. "Of course."

Lifting the second lantern, she searched in the closet area and found several tanks. She did a quick count, then grabbed one to take closer to the bed."

"There are seven there, including this one," she told Mrs. Peterson.

The older woman looked up at her with worry etched across her face. "I worry that won't be enough."

At that moment, Jenny froze. "Enough?"

"To get through the storm."

"But what about the generator?"

She shook her head. "It's old and crotchety. I don't know if Ben can get it going."

"Then what do we do?"

Mrs. Peterson's gaze dropped to her husband's sleeping face. "Pray."

Jenny's heart seized in anguish for the woman. "Is he okay?"

She looked back up at Jenny and shook her head. "He's been sleeping since early this afternoon. I sensed the big storm coming and sent home the help. I knew Harold would prefer to go without nurses hovering over him."

Jenny sucked in a quick breath. "He's dying?"

She nodded and whispered, "Yes. Not yet, but his time is short."

"I should leave you to be alone with him."

The older woman reached for Jenny's hand and tugged.

"No. Sit with me, please. Bring that desk chair over here and stay with me while I sit with Harold. Can you do that, sweetie?"

"Of course." Jenny retrieved the chair and positioned it closer. "If you are sure."

"I am." She laid her hand on Jenny's knee, looked long into her eyes, and sighed. "I thought I wanted to be alone with Harold when the time came, but for some reason, right now, I want company."

Jenny nodded and placed her hand over Mrs. Peterson's. "I'm happy to stay here with you. And honored."

"One day, before you realize it, this day will come for you and Ben. One of you will pass before the other, and one of you will be alone. You are lucky, Jenny. You found each other when you were young, and you and Ben are going to have a long life together. I know it."

Jenny sighed. "I'm not so sure, Mrs. Peterson."

"Call me Elaine." She patted her hand. "We need to be on a first name basis here, sweetie. It's going to be a long night. Now, tell me why you are not sure about you and Ben. I can clearly see the love he has for you in his eyes."

Yes, Jenny could see that too.

"I..." Jenny hesitated. "I'm not sure it's the time or place to discuss my problems, Mrs., um, Elaine."

Elaine Peterson studied Jenny's face for a moment, then looked back to her husband. Taking his hand in hers, she brought it up to her lips and kissed it. "There's never a good time to discuss some things."

That statement hit home immediately and tangled with her heart. *Never a good time to discuss some things.* Had she avoided talking to her parents about her feelings? About college? About Ben? Was she somehow at fault with her family issues?

"That's very true. And something I need to think about."

Elaine looked up and smiled. But beyond the sparkle in her pupils, and the thin-lipped grin spreading across her face, Jenny also saw fatigue in her eyes, and the slight quiver of her lower lip.

TEN

BEN HAD some difficulty with the generator. He figured it hadn't been started in a couple of years. And while it rested on a covered part of the porch, he needed to move it away from the house, where there would be no threat of fumes getting inside. Where to, also posed a problem, with the snow piling up. But he got it off the porch and under the overhang of a shed several feet away. Luckily, the heavy-duty extension cord reached that far.

He'd popped inside once to tell Mrs. Peterson and Jenny that he had to do some fiddling with the starter, and that it would be several minutes more before he would have things running.

He found the pair in the bedroom chatting.

"We'll be fine for a while. Harold has at least four to five hours of oxygen in the tanks," Mrs. Peterson said. "I'm sure you'll have it going before then. I'll only fret if we need to rely on tanks past then."

"I surely hope that is not the case," Ben told her, then worried that he'd be able to keep his promise. Promises seemed easily broken these days. He glanced at Jenny. "Are you okay?"

She rose and stepped toward the bedroom door, picking up a lantern on her way. She motioned for him to step into the hallway.

He followed her.

She turned toward him. The worry etched into her face frightened him.

"Oh, Ben. This is awful."

"What?"

"Mr. Peterson is dying. She sent the nurses home."

"What? Are you okay in there?"

Jenny nodded frantically. "I'm fine. She wants me to stay with her, and in some small, strange way, I want to be with her too. I don't think she has anyone else."

"They never had children."

Sucking in a breath, Jenny stared into the room. "It's sad."

Ben touched her arm to get her attention. "I'm going back outside. I'll be in as soon as I get that rickety thing running."

"Is it really that bad?"

"Bad enough."

Jenny and Elaine talked in whispers while Harold slept. She was still having a difficult time calling her Elaine instead of Mrs. Peterson.

"Being called Mrs. Peterson just makes me feel damned old," she confessed to Jenny. "Even though I am old. I'll be eighty-two next month, you know."

"I would have guessed you were in your seventies," Jenny teased

Elaine cackled then. "Oh sweetie. You are a hoot."

It was nice hearing her laugh. She wondered if there had been much room in her life lately for laughter.

Elaine looked at Jenny. "You and Ben make a lovely couple."

Glancing off, Jenny studied a picture over the bed, avoiding her comment. It looked to be one of those aerial pictures of a farm—perhaps this farm, she wasn't sure. It had been taken some time ago, she guessed. She'd seen one of those before, at her grandparents' home—her father's parents—in the country. They'd not gone there much in recent years, but she remembered the picture perfectly.

"Jenny?"

She looked at Elaine. "I'm sorry. You were saying?"

"Your wedding. When are you getting married?"

Hesitantly, she debated how to respond. "Well, we were on our way to the judge when the storm hit. I guess we've postponed."

"You guess?"

Jenny shrugged. "Well, it can't happen today, that's for certain."

Elaine studied her. "Are you unsure about this marriage, Jenny?"

"Well, of course. No. Sure. It's complicated. I..." The words tumbled out. Jenny knew she wasn't making sense.

Elaine reached for her hand and tucked it between both of hers. "Tell me. Tell me everything."

With a sigh, Jenny dove in. "It's just that.... I wish things had gone better with my parents. That they understood."

"They are against the marriage?"

"My father, yes. I think my mother would come around if not for him. But I haven't had a chance to talk with her."

Elaine nodded. "You should find that time."

"I know."

"That said, you are an adult, right? You can make your own decisions. Why do you feel you need their blessing?

"I think it's because I've always done everything to please them. Grades, and so on, that's what I've always done. It makes me ache inside to think that I've done something that will affect my relationship with my parents for the rest of my life."

"And what about your relationship with Ben?"

That statement stunned Jenny a little. "I didn't think of it in that way."

"You should. You love him. Right?"

"Oh, more than anything."

"Then that's all you need. One relationship is not more important than the other. You just need to figure out how to make it work."

"But—"

Elaine laid a finger on her lips. "Sh. No buts. If there is love, true love, you cannot deny it. You can try to push it away. You can try to reason with it. But if it's true, it will refuse to be denied, and it will fight its way back to you."

Jenny thought about that for a minute. "Could it really be that simple?"

"No. It's not simple at all, Jenny. I have some beliefs about love if you want to hear them."

"I do." She nodded and was thinking there was something rather serendipitous about this day and evening, and them landing here at the Petersons. "Please?"

"I don't believe you meddle with first love," Elaine began. "First love is powerfully strong. There is a bond there that I believe never goes away. In fact, I know that firsthand.

"When that love gets disrupted, it affects the rest of your life. Your choices, your subsequent loves, and relationships, and more. I don't think you even realize it at the time—until your one true love finally comes back to you."

Jenny watched the older woman wind her fingers with her husband's as she thumbed his knuckles, and then adjusted his oxygen tube.

The way she looked at him... They had something special. Powerful. She could feel it.

Jenny felt like a spectator to a private moment that she wasn't sure she would witness.

She glanced off, and her gaze landed on an old picture on the dresser.

"Were you high school sweethearts?"

Elaine's gaze lifted from her husband to the picture. It was an old picture of a couple of teenagers, all dressed up in fancy clothes. Made of cardboard, the frame holding the picture was frayed and bent on the edges. Jenny watched a slow smile travel over Elaine's face.

"We were in high school," she started, her voice a mere whisper. "He was my boyfriend, and a year older than me. That year, he was a junior and I was a sophomore. He asked me out through a friend of his, and I have to say I'd never given the boy a second glance. But that day, I suppose knowing he had some sort of interest in me, things changed. We started exchanging notes throughout the day. He'd smile shyly as we passed in the hall. Eventually, we went out, and from then on, it was just the two of us for nearly three years. Then he graduated."

"And you broke up?"

She looked at her. "Yes, but not because of him graduating. My mother came between us. I suppose she was only protecting me, in a way. But she meddled between us until I questioned the relationship and started to think what life would be like without him once he went off to college.

"The breakup was bad. Poor guy, he had quite a time of it. He tried and tried to get me back that summer. Did anything he could think of to impress me. New clothes. New car. Letters. Wanted to take me out to fancy places to eat.

"But I had shut down. I think it was easier for me to shut him out of my life, than to deal with my mother. At least that's what I thought at the time."

Her gaze drifted off for a moment, then she looked back at her dying husband and stroked his face. "He's unconscious, you know. Not just sleeping. I gave him strong painkillers and a sedative before you and Ben arrived. That's one reason why he is sleeping so soundly. Earlier in the day, it was the hospice nurses that I sent home. I wanted alone time with Harold before he passed on. Our last Christmas Eve together."

Jenny stood. "Oh my, Elaine. Really and truly, Ben and I shouldn't be here. We are imposing and I—"

Elaine grasped her hand. "No, you should be here. You and your young man... You are so much in love, I can see it. And I love feeling the power of that between you. It reminds me so much of my own first love. Love is powerful, Jenny. Never forget that. Promise me. With it, you can get through anything."

Tears stung Jenny's eyelids as Elaine stared at her with intent. Nodding, she whispered, "I promise."

"I wish I'd been strong enough to stand up to my mother. In the end, our relationship was never the same either. I always blamed her, and I regret that."

Jenny squeezed Elaine's hand. "I understand. I truly do."

"This thing has come between the two of you. Don't let it Jenny."

"I don't want it to, truly."

"Resolve the issue with your parents. Perhaps that will free up your mind and you'll know exactly what to do next."

Jenny nodded. "Perhaps." She wondered about that. "You are right. I need to face it head on."

Elaine smiled. "There are so many things in life we need to face head on. Don't avoid them. Face them and conquer them."

Leaning in, Jenny gave the old woman a hug. "Thank you, Elaine." Pulling back, she smiled and studied her face. "You didn't finish the story. What happened to you and your high school beaux? Your first, young love?"

Elaine smiled broadly then and looked lovingly at Harold. "Oh, he's right here. Harold was my one true love, Jenny. We went our separate ways. We each married another, but neither of us had children. After several years, I divorced my husband. Harold lost his wife in a car accident.

"We didn't find each other again until nearly forty years had passed—but we've been together ever since. There are days I mourn those decades we were apart. The life we missed experiencing together. A wedding. Children. Growing old over time. But now... I'm only happy we are together. I often wished I had not listened to my mother and had run off with Harold all those years ago, like he wanted me to do."

Jenny's heart swelled as she watched the Peterson couple. Elaine lovingly stroked Harold's face and cooed soft words to him. The strong bond, the love they shared, had carried them through time and would end here tonight. Sniffling, Jenny glanced off toward the young teenage couple in the picture on the dresser.

Elaine spoke quietly. "Having you here, right now, Jenny. Well. It helped me to remember how much Harold and I loved each other as teenagers, and how even though we were separated by decades, I'm so grateful we found our way back to each other, and that we will have these final hours together."

She stroked his head again, then leaned in to kiss him on the cheek. "If there is one thing I've learned in life, it's when to hold on, and when to let go. Think about that. Is it time to hold on to Ben with everything you have? Or is it time to let go?"

After a moment, she waved Jenny off, and carefully climbed into bed beside the love of her life. As Jenny quietly left the room, she noticed Elaine's dampening cheeks.

Time to let go?

In the hallway, she met Ben coming in from the back door, carrying a thick extension cord.

"Ben. Oh, Ben." She rushed toward him. "Where are you going?"

"To plug this into Harold's oxygen machine."

Jenny grasped his biceps, shaking her head. "No, wait. Give Elaine a minute. She...." Her words trailed off, and suddenly, Jenny sobbed, and tears rolled down her cheeks. "She's letting go. Harold is.... Oh, Ben. It's so terribly sad."

Ben lifted her chin with his forefinger. "Jenny? What is going on? Are you okay?"

"No. Yes. Yes, I'm okay. Ben, I'm so sorry. I was wrong. I've messed everything up. I love you so much and I don't want us to be apart. I'm not ready to let you go. Ever. I still want to marry you. I want very much to be your wife. If you'll have me."

Ben dropped the heavy extension cord and grabbed Jenny up into a bear hug that she never wanted to end.

ELEVEN

EARLY THE NEXT MORNING, Jenny blinked herself awake, squinting against a beam of sunlight shining in the window, and pushed herself into an upright position on the sofa. Ben was still asleep, curled up against the sofa arm, a blanket wrapped around his shoulders. She remembered hunting for that blanket the night before and tucking it around them while they slept in each other's arms in front of the stove.

It didn't take either of them long to fall asleep.

A quick glance at the anniversary clock on the mantel told her the time was just after seven in the morning. She stepped toward the front door and peeked out the window. The morning was still and bright, with several inches of sparkling snow blanketing the area. The good news was that the aftermath of the storm didn't look as bad as she feared. The generator was still running outside, and she could hear the hum of the oxygen machine in Harold's and Elaine's bedroom. Ben had plugged it in for Elaine a few hours ago.

She wondered how Elaine was doing.

Ben stirred on the sofa, catching her eye. "Good morning," he murmured. "What time is it?"

"Early. But the snow has stopped, and it doesn't look too bad out there."

"Great." Ben rose and stumbled toward the door. "That's a very good sign. I wonder if I can dig us out this morning so we can get back home?"

"I hope so," Jenny said. "But I don't know about leaving Elaine."

Ben rubbed his chin. "I know. We will figure something out. I don't like the idea of leaving her alone with Harold in this condition. I wonder when the hospice nurses are coming back?"

"Elaine probably knows."

Gathering her into his arms, Ben peered down into her eyes, a serious look on his face. "Good morning. I love you."

She smiled. "Good morning to you. I love you back."

Leaning in for a quick kiss, Ben hugged her tighter. "Merry Christmas," he added after a moment.

Jenny pulled back. "Goodness. You're right. It is Christmas day."

"Yep. And we were supposed to be in the mountains today on our honeymoon."

"What? Really?"

He nodded, touching his nose to hers. "If we can dig out early, I'm wondering if we can make it by tonight?"

"To the mountains?"

"Umhm. For our honeymoon."

"But..." Jenny searched his face. "But we'd have to get married first to have a honeymoon and there is the snow and...."

He silenced her with a kiss. Jenny relaxed and let him nibble her lips for a long, sweet moment. "Oh..."

He spoke softly between kisses. "Marry me. Today. Jenny

Anderson. On Christmas day. Please? Put me out of my misery."

Jenny reluctantly let go of the last kiss, stared into his eyes, and whispered. "If anyone can make it happen today, Ben Matthews, it's you. We have the whole day ahead of us. Yes. I love you. Let's get married."

Stepping back, Ben cocked his head and studied her. "Do you want to try to clear things up with your parents first?"

Jenny thought about that, taking a big breath in, and exhaling slowly. "You know, I do need to have a discussion with them. Elaine and I talked about that last night. But I also need to do what is best for us. And today? We need to focus on getting married. I'm not procrastinating the inevitable, I'm simply putting our relationship first. I hope that is okay with you?"

A slinky grin crept across Ben's face, then burst into a big smile. Reaching for her, he grasped her forearms and tugged her closer. "That, my love, is absolutely fine with me. In fact, it's perfect."

Leaning in, he took her lips in another slow and sultry kiss. Breaking away, he gave her a silly grin and said, "There's more where that came from...later." His eyebrows waggled as he teased.

Jenny punched his shoulder and grinned. "Oh, you!"

Abruptly, the humming sound in the bedroom stopped, and a strange silence filled the space around them. Ben and Jenny froze and looked toward the hallway as Elaine stepped from the shadows and into the room.

"Mrs. Peterson?" Ben asked, stepping toward her. "Is everything all right?"

She shook her head. "No. Nothing is going to be right again, for the rest of my life."

Jenny rushed to Elaine and wrapped her arms around the

older woman, who suddenly seemed a lot frailer than she had the night before. "Oh, Elaine. I'm so sorry. Come sit over here."

She helped her to the sofa where they sat, side by side.

"I let go." Elaine whispered, leaning her head against Jenny's shoulder. "I finally let go, and he slipped away in the night, and I'm not sure what to do next."

"We'll help," Jenny told her, rubbing her shoulder.

"I mean with my life. How do I live without him?"

Jenny hugged her closer. "I don't know the answer to that. I suppose you have to take it one day at a time."

The older woman turned in Jenny's arms then and whispered. "Hold on to him with everything you have, Jenny, for as long as you can. You won't regret it. Not one second. I promise you."

Jenny saw the pain in Elaine Peterson's eyes. "I promise you I will."

Elaine sighed and leaned into Jenny. She patted her knee and whispered. "You're a good, good girl. I like you, Jenny Anderson. I hope you marry the Matthews boy." In the background, the lights flickered, and Ben said something about a truck coming up the driveway.

With the help of some neighbors down the road, Ben dug the truck out in a couple of hours. While that happened, a few locals with plows on the front of their trucks worked to clear a path down the country road for traffic. He was amazed that the aftermath of the snow squall the night before was not worse. He supposed he and Jenny had gotten into the thick of it, and things must have dissipated during the night.

Jenny stayed inside with Mrs. Peterson and waited for

people to come and help with Harold. The phone at the house was still dead, but one neighbor helping Ben had service at home, so he called hospice, who then called the funeral home and other authorities.

Ben also asked him to call his parents and let them know they were okay, where they were, and that they would be back home soon.

A couple of hours later, they were ready to leave. Jenny felt terrible leaving Mrs. Peterson alone at the house and wanted her to come with them.

"No," Mrs. Peterson told them. "I'm not going anywhere today. The hospice nurse offered to stay for a while, but I told her no. I'm tired and I want to sleep. I need some quiet time to reflect and think. I will be fine. I have everything I need."

"Except for a phone," Ben reminded her.

"Except for that. And that could be a blessing." She grinned slightly and herded them toward the front of the house. "I expect once word gets out that people will stop by later today. Now, it's time for you the two of you to take control of your own lives and get on with your plans." She stared first at Jenny, then Ben. "You do have plans. Right?"

Jenny smiled. "Yes. We have plans."

"Good. Then get to them. I'm going to take a nap."

Ben nodded and put his arm around Jenny. "Someone will be by to check on you later."

"Of course. Now, skedaddle."

"Yes, Ma'am," Ben said.

"Don't Ma'am me," Elaine told him. "Makes me feel like an old woman."

Ben laughed. Jenny hugged and kissed her goodbye.

Thirty minutes later, the couple pulled up to the Matthews' home. An additional vehicle parked in the driveway was the first thing Jenny noticed.

She gasped. "Ben. That's my parents' car."

He slowed the truck and braked. "What?"

"My parents. They are here."

Shoving the gearshift into park, Ben turned to her. "Jenny, look at me."

She did. "Why are they here?"

Ben exhaled. "I don't know. Take a breath. Let's think about this a second before going inside."

Jenny nodded. "Yes."

"Obviously, they are here because they care about you. Enough so, it looks like, to brave a snowstorm and make their way to a place they've never been, and to see people they have barely met."

"That's true."

Ben stared harder into her eyes. "The bottom line here is, Jenny, that this changes nothing between you and me. Right?"

She glanced at her parents' car, then back to Ben. "It changes everything."

He jerked back. "How so?"

"I'm going to fix it. I'm going to make it right. Right now. Today. It's something I should have done long ago, but I need to tell my parents exactly how I feel, that I love you, I hate school, and that I love them too and want to keep them in my life."

"And we are still getting married."

"You bet we are. Ben Matthews, I'm holding on to you for the rest of my life. I hope you are ready for that."

He gathered her into his arms. "Sweetheart, I can't wait."

TWELVE

AS JENNY WALKED UP to the Matthews' home, she wondered what kind of situation waited for her inside the house. Bracing herself for whatever onslaught her parents wanted to unleash, she also hoped her father would be a bit more reserved since he was out of his element, and in someone else's home.

"I can handle this," she said aloud as they stepped onto the porch.

"You got this, Jenny." Ben squeezed her hand. "Remember, I love you, and we are in this together."

With a deep breath and exhale—from them both—Ben pushed open the door.

"Jennifer! Thank God." Her father stood in the entry, taking a hesitant half-step forward. Her mother stood slightly to his right, wringing her hands. On the left were Ben's parents. The looks on their faces were ones of concern.

"Hi Dad. Mom." Tears stung the back of her eyelids. She didn't want to cry. It was the last thing she wanted to do right now, but she feared the tears may spill, anyway.

"Oh, honey..." Her dad rushed forward and swept her into his arms. "I'm so happy to see you."

His big bear hug felt like coming home. She'd not had one of those in a very long time. Holding back her tears was no longer possible.

"I'm sorry, Dad." She sniffled. "I never meant to upset you so, but it seemed it was the only way I could do what was right for me."

"No. I'm the one who is sorry." He pulled back and studied her, then continued. "I'm the one who caused all the friction and made it difficult for you, and for Ben. It's my fault, not yours. I'm a stubborn old man. I've been on a royal tear for the past few years, mostly because I'm unhappy with myself, but I finally got set straight the night you left."

Puzzled, Jenny glanced from him to her mother. "How? What do you mean?"

He followed her gaze to his wife.

Her mother stepped forward. "Well, I had a few things to say after Ben left the house two nights ago, and we watched you both drive away. Things I should have said a long time ago but didn't. Watching you and Ben drive away, and knowing he told you to never come back. Well. I told him I was leaving too. That finally got his attention."

"Mom? Seriously?"

She nodded. "Yes. And I'm sorry I didn't do it sooner. I should have stood up more for you and your feelings. I should have listened, and I didn't. So, your father and I are both at fault here."

She moved closer to Jenny, brushed her fingertips over her cheek, and stroked her hair. "We set out for Dickens yesterday morning and figured once we got here, we would find Ben's parents. We were right—small town indeed—all we had to do was pull up to the gazebo in town and ask the first person who came along. Within a few minutes, we had an address and a phone number. We called and told them we were on our way to meet them, and I must say they have been very accommodating with our last-minute arrival."

Maureen Matthews stepped into the crowd. "And we've had a lovely visit, Jenny. I've enjoyed meeting your parents very much. You are a lucky girl."

A lucky girl. Elaine Peterson said the same thing.

She supposed she was. "I think I need a moment to process all of this."

"Take your time, honey," her father said. "None of us are going anywhere for a while."

That was for certain. "So, you're not here to try and convince me to go back home?"

Her mother shook her head. "No. We came, hopefully, for your wedding."

"Our wedding? You want to come?"

"We all do," Maureen added, tossing a glance at Calvin, and hooking her hand in the crook of his elbow. "Right?"

He nodded. "We would love to be there. If you and Ben agree."

Ben? Turning, she caught his eye as he stood barely a foot away from her. Just like he'd said he would, he was right by her side. "We do, right?"

"Yes. Definitely." He grinned and put his arm around her.

Jenny's father interjected. "We thought we'd spend a little time in Dickens after the festivities. We hear it's a great little village and we want to know more about the town where our daughter is going to live. Besides, we haven't been on a vacation in years and it's high time."

Her mother edged forward. "But first, the wedding. Just to clarify, there is going to be a wedding, albeit a small one, isn't there?"

Jenny looked at Ben. He put his arm around her. "Yes, Mrs. Anderson. There is going to be a wedding."

A few hoots and hollers went up from the parents.

"I'm Katherine, by the way," she said to Ben, then gave him a hug. "I should have done that long ago."

"And I'm Craig." He shot Ben an intense stare and put out his hand.

Ben gave him a slight stare back, then shook it. Jenny noticed the shake was firm, from both men.

She took another deep breath. "Dad, can we talk? You, me, and mom?" She looked at Ben and reached for his hand. "And Ben, too."

Her father dropped his chin in a nod. "Of course. I'd like that."

Calvin Matthews stepped forward. "My office is right down the hall if you want privacy." He pointed. "Jenny knows the way."

Dropping Ben's hand, Jenny gave her soon-to-be father-in-law a hug. "That would be perfect. Thank you."

Ben sidled up beside Jenny. "I have just one thing to say first though." He glanced at his watch. "If there is going to be a Christmas wedding today, I need to check in with the judge and make sure she's available."

With a twinkle in her eye, Maureen said, "Oh, no worries there, son. She'll be here at six. That gives us roughly seven hours to get ready."

"Piece of cake," Katherine Anderson stepped closer to Maureen. "Where's your phone? Let's get moving." She glanced at Jenny. "But after we talk, of course."

"What?" Ben's gaze darted between the two moms. "What have you done?"

Maureen smiled and kissed her son on the cheek. "What mothers do."

Jenny smiled and hugged her mom. Then to Ben, she said, "Let them do their thing. Besides, the train has left the station. It's out of our control."

The mood in the office a few minutes later was a little more somber. Jenny leaned against the desk and crossed her arms, hoping she had her parents' full attention. They stood opposite her, their gazes fixed on her.

"Dad, Mom, I'm not really sure where to start because I'm not sure how everything got so tangled up, but I'm glad we are talking."

"We are too, honey." Her mom grinned nervously and glanced at her dad.

Jenny hoped she was on the right track here. Things were finally smoothing over. She didn't want to upset her father again.

Her gaze darted back and forth between her parents. "I should have told you long ago, Dad. I tried, many times, but I couldn't get all the words I wanted to say out of my mouth. I don't want to be a lawyer. I have never wanted to be a lawyer. I didn't want to disappoint you, so I sort of went with it."

"We knew that, sweetheart," her mother said. "Deep down. We were just avoiding it, I think. And we will admit we had unfair expectations. Candy was so easy. She knew what she wanted in life. There were times we just didn't know about you."

That was true about her sister. Her ambitions were well known since she was in elementary school. While she was laser-focused on her law degree, Jenny floundered from this to that, entertaining all sorts of ideas about what her future might look like.

"Speaking of Candy... Is she here?"

Katherine shook her head. "No. She has an interview tomorrow, so she is home preparing."

"Oh, that makes sense. I figured she might be mourning the fact that I was getting married first."

"Well, that too," Katherine said. "You know your sister."

"That I do." Jenny noticed her dad was pacing a little. "Dad, what do we need to clear up about school? Are you okay with me not going to law school, so I can explore an art career?"

"Frankly, I know nothing about this art business. How do you make money at painting pictures? You need to get me up to speed."

Jenny laughed. "Most artists I know are called starving artists for a reason. It's hard to make a living by making art. But with me, it's not all about making a living. I need to paint. To create stuff. It's who I am. And I want to learn more and more about it and live my life in a creative way—degree or no degree."

Her dad nodded, then looked to Ben. "And since you are going to be a married couple, are you okay with this?"

Ben smiled. "Why not? I'm more than okay, Mr. Anderson, um, Craig. I understand what's in Jenny's heart and soul. I make a decent living at the hardware store. One day, it will be mine. Right now, I live in the apartment above it, rent free. Jenny and I will stay there while we save to buy a house. There is a room in the back that is perfect for a studio. That space is Jenny's to do with as she pleases."

Her father contemplated Ben's words, then turned to her. "Your mother and I have talked, Jenny, and we will foot the bill for art school, if that is what you want."

Jenny's gaze bounced from her father to her mother. "I may take you up on that, but I need a little time to figure things out. I'll likely do community college or correspondence courses for now. I need to check into what is available in this area. Then down the road, we can discuss more." Hesitantly, she moved forward and hugged her father. "Thank you."

Her mother tapped her fingertips on the desktop. "You know, I have things to do. Have we wrapped this up yet? We have a wedding to plan and literally no time to do it." She turned for the door.

"Wait. There is one more thing I want to say before we leave here, just for the record. I want to make sure that you both, Dad and Mom, have no qualms about Ben and me getting married. We are getting married, regardless, but I also want to make sure you understand that I want you both in our lives, too. I love you and it's unfair to make me choose between my family and Ben and his family. Are we good there?"

Her dad smiled. "Are you sure you don't want to be a lawyer? That was a pretty convincing speech."

Jenny hugged him. "I learned from the best."

Her father's expression grew serious. "Jennifer, I have a lot of work to do on myself. I realize I was a domineering old man —I was turning into my father, a man I always said I didn't want to be like. I didn't realize how much until I got so angry with Ben the other evening. I'm working on it. Okay? In the meantime, the answer to your question is yes. We are good here. Whatever you want, I want."

Jenny's eyes teared up. "I love you, Dad. One more question."

"Yes?"

"Will you give me away tonight?"

This time, Craig Anderson didn't hold back his emotion, choking back tears. "As long as I'm not giving you away forever."

Jenny let go of a long-held sigh. Leaning up on tiptoes, she gave her dad a kiss. "You're not getting rid of me that easily."

Her mother sighed. "Are we finished here, you two? Wedding? Time is short."

Laughing, her father glanced at Ben. "Can you stick around? Let's let the womenfolk do their thing. I think we need a chat, just you and me."

"I look forward to it," Ben said.

Jenny peeked around Maureen to look at the clock on the dresser in her bedroom. In an hour she would be married. "Are you sure Ben is okay? I've not seen him since this morning in Calvin's office."

"He's fine, Jenny. I promise," Maureen said. "Besides, the groom is not supposed to see the bride the day of the wedding, and we've already tempted fate in that regard earlier in the day."

"Well, that was unavoidable." Jenny looked at herself in the mirror, turning this way, and the other. Curling iron in hand, Maureen curled her hair into long tendrils. "That looks pretty, Maureen. Thank you."

"I was thinking maybe we could try pinning some of these pieces up once I get all the curls."

"Oh, I like that idea too. You're good at this."

"I used to work in a salon years ago. You should have seen me during prom week! This curling iron was stuck to my hand like a third appendage. I'm rusty though."

"Well, I like it!"

Her future mother-in-law bent down to look in the mirror too, their faces side-by-side. "You're going to make a beautiful bride. I'm so happy for you and Ben."

Jenny returned her smile in the mirror. "I'm happy for all of us."

Katherine swept in from the hallway. "Well, I made all the calls on the list you gave me, Maureen. You're right. The people in this town are so friendly and giving. Not one person refused to help us out, even on Christmas day. Do you think that would happen in Philadelphia? No. The only thing I had to promise to anyone was a piece of cake to the florist. I can't believe they still had poinsettias."

"What about the bakery?"

Katherine checked something off on her list. "All done. Leslie's Bakery was happy to whip up something. She said it would not be her usual wedding cake fare—because those generally take a couple of days to create—but she said she could wing a small cake with already baked layers she had on hand."

"Great."

"And the photographer?"

"Out of town. However, when I talked with the florist about the flowers, she told me about a woman who is just getting her business started. So, I called her, but she has little kids and well, Christmas, but she told me to call a man named Rand Carpenter, who lives in another town, I think, but close. Thankfully, he said he could do it and will be here at five-thirty."

"Well, thank goodness. You really had your work cut out for you. I think that's everything."

Jenny cleared her throat. "Maybe not everything."

The women stared. "What? We have forgotten nothing. I'm sure of it."

Jenny looked down at herself. She stood before them in jeans, an over-sized, navy-blue V-neck sweater, and her Eastland's. "I don't have a dress. Ben and I hadn't planned on anything fancy, just a quickie wedding at the judge's house. I didn't pack a dress in my backpack."

Looking up, she caught her mother's eye, and saw the mist

in them. "No worries, honey," she said softly. "I have you covered."

Katherine left the room and Jenny and Maureen exchanged glances. Very soon, she returned with a garment bag on a hanger. Katherine positioned the bag on the bed and unzipped. With a flick of her wrist, she pulled out a cream-colored, sleek and chic, wedding dress. No sequins, no ruffles or bows, no lace, no pearls—just a classy, off-the-shoulder wedding dress that looked perfect to Jenny.

"This is your dress, Mom."

She nodded. "It's yours now. Try it on?"

"Seriously? I've wanted to try on this dress since I was a little girl, and you never would let me." Stripping down to her underwear, and with the help of the women, Jenny slipped into the gown. Perfect.

"Well, I wanted to wait for this moment, sweetheart. Oh, my. You are stunning."

Jenny spun slowly in front of the mirror. The women admired her.

"It fits her perfectly."

"It's beautiful."

"Do we need to tuck anything anywhere?"

"No. It's a picture-perfect fit. What do you think, Jenny?"

"I think..." She stood still and looked at herself in the mirror. "I think I'm getting married today."

"That you are."

Katherine took her daughter in her arms then and hugged her tight. Maureen was right behind her. Jenny was pretty sure both women were crying.

The knock came at the door.

"Yes?" Maureen called out.

Calvin answered back. "Grace is here, honey."

Katherine glanced at her watch. "That's the judge," she said to Katherine. "Already? Where has the time gone?"

Jenny escaped the clutches of the two moms and smoothed her dress down while she took one long and heartfelt look in the mirror. This was her wedding day. She was marrying Ben.

Exhaling long, she let the moment wash over her. "I *am* going to marry that boy today," she whispered, then stepped away from the mirror.

"You two go ahead of me. I want a minute, and then send Daddy up."

Katherine and Maureen left in a flitter.

THIRTEEN

WHEN JENNY STEPPED down the staircase on her father's arm, joining the family in the living room, Ben thought his heart would literally jump out of his chest. Jenny—his Jenny—was a beautiful bride. Stunning. And wearing a sophisticated wedding dress he'd no idea she even possessed.

Suddenly, he was glad his father had insisted he wear his suit.

Smiling shyly as she turned the corner, she slowly approached him. When she stood by his side and faced the judge with him, he had to remind himself not to lock his knees so he wouldn't get lightheaded and pass out right there in front of everyone.

But his knees were shaking anyway, and so were his hands.

Jenny reached to her right and tangled her fingers with his left hand, casually. He calmed somewhat.

Leaning to his left, he whispered, "You are so beautiful. I love you, Jenny Anderson."

She met his gaze back and smiled. "I love you too," she said on a breath. "Always."

The wedding was small, and that was exactly the way they had planned it, although a little larger than the elopement they thought they were going to get. Jenny's parents stood to her left. His parents stood to his right. Charlotte and her crew sat on the sofa behind them all.

Suddenly, the front door swung open, and a cold whiff of air ruffled throughout the room. Everyone turned to watch Jenny's sister, Candy, stumble in the door.

She blew out a breath. "Whew. Looks like I made it in the nick of time." She approached Jenny, gave her a hug and a smile, then settled into a chair close to her parents.

The judge cleared her throat. She said some words. Ben heard them but didn't comprehend a single one of them. He grasped Jenny's hand tighter with his sweaty left hand.

"Who gives this woman today?"

Craig stepped forward. "Her mother and I, your honor."

The judge looked at Jenny's dad and grinned. "Thank you, but we're not in court room, Mr. Anderson."

A giggle or two went up in the room and Ben relaxed a little. He looked at Jenny, who was also smiling.

The judge grinned and continued. The ceremony was short and sweet.

They exchanged rings.

Both Jenny and Ben said their vows.

"I promise to always hold on to you, Ben Matthews, and never let you go. I will love you until our days are through."

"And I promise you, Jenny Anderson, that I will love and take care of you, cherish you, and be thankful for you, all the days of my life."

There was a brief pause, and Ben took advantage of the silence and the moment to stare into Jenny's eyes. Six months ago, he could never have guessed this day would happen. His mind drifted back to that day on the beach when he first spotted her.

Her with her big, bronze eyes staring back at him.

Him being drawn to her like a nothing he'd ever before experienced, just wanting to know more about her.

"I've loved you from the first moment I saw you, Jenny," he whispered.

She smiled through misty tears. "That day we met, I went back to the beach house, and told myself that I might just marry you one day. And now, well…"

Ben's chest swelled. He was so happy. So full of love for her. And so ready for the rest of their lives together.

The judge cleared her throat again. "By the power bestowed upon me by this state, I now pronounce you man and wife. Ben Matthews, kiss your bride before you spontaneously combust or keel over into a quivery puddle of gelatin on the living room floor."

Jenny laughed and threw her arms around his neck. Tears and cheers sounded in the room. Ben gathered her close, leaned in, and took her lips in their first kiss as a married couple. And he enjoyed every…last…second…of it.

Once more, the front door swung open wide, a gust of wind played peek-a-boo in the room, and everyone turned that way. Elaine Peterson slowly ambled inside on the arm of one of Dickens' local police officers, smiling. "Well, looks like I nearly missed it," she said.

Jenny and Ben rushed forward.

"Mrs. Peterson. What in the world are you doing here?" Ben asked. "We didn't expect you. It's been such a long day for you."

She grasped his forearm to steady herself, then glanced at the officer. "I'm fine now, Joel. Come back in thirty minutes if you will."

He nodded at her, then tipped his hat to the rest of the room and left.

Mrs. Peterson scanned the crowd. "He's my neighbor. Hey, it's not every day you can catch a ride with a hunky policeman, right?"

More laughter skittered through the room.

Jenny hugged the older woman. "I'm so glad you are here, but you surely didn't have to come. How are you holding up today?" She led her to a chair. "Why don't you sit?"

Mrs. Peterson waved her off. "I'm fine. I had a long nap. It's been both a sad day, and a happy day. But I couldn't let it go by before seeing that the two of you were married. You've been on my mind all afternoon."

"I've been thinking of you too, Elaine," Jenny told her.

The older woman smiled and patted her hand. "Before I forget about it, I have something for the two of you." She pulled a manilla envelope out of the purse hanging on her arm. "Ben, you're a good man. And Jenny, I just met you, but you are perfect for Ben. I know you will have a long and beautiful life together. Open this later, after I'm gone. I just wanted you to have it today. And let me see those rings, you two."

Ben took the envelope. They showed her their left hands.

Elaine Peterson smiled. "All right. Then this is a good day— a very good day—after all."

Much later, after Mrs. Peterson had left, the cake was devoured, champagne flowed, and the family wedding pictures taken, Ben and Jenny changed into travel clothes and grabbed their luggage so they could get to the mountains for their honeymoon.

As they embraced family and gave kisses at the front door,

Jenny spied the manilla envelope sitting on the table by the door. She gasped Ben's arm.

"Ben? We forgot about the envelope from Elaine."

"Oh, that's right." He stepped to the table and retrieved it. "Should we see what's in it?"

Jenny nodded. "Yes. Let's do."

The family gathered around while Ben opened the envelope. He pulled out several pieces of paper, shuffled through them, then lifted his gaze to look at Jenny. "There is a letter and some legal papers."

Puzzled, Jenny stepped closer. "What?"

Ben began reading the short letter....

D*ear Ben and Jenny,*

Thank you for being with me last night when Harold left me, and for all you and Jenny did to help me through the night. The most important thing you both did was to remind me how much in love Harold and I were when we were kids—I saw it in the two of you. Last night, I needed that.

Now, I'm an old woman and I'm not going to be around much longer. As you know, Harold and I had no children. Holly Hill Farm was in Harold's family for a couple of generations, but there is no more family on his side to pass this beautiful farm on to.

So, I am giving it to you. Upon my death, Holly Hill Farm belongs to the two of you. I've managed to get paperwork signed and taken care of today. Yes, even on Christmas Day. It's my wedding gift to you on this very special Christmas. We may need to meet with the attorneys again next week, but this is my intent.

Enjoy the home, the land, and please, please have children and raise them there. It's something I was never able to do. I want to know that one day, children's voices will again ring in the halls of that big house.

Hold on to each other, Ben and Jenny. Hold on until you can't. Only then, do you let go.

I am forever grateful for you both.

Elaine Peterson

EPILOGUE

EIGHTEEN MONTHS LATER, Holly Hill Inn

"I can't believe you would even consider opening the Inn while you're in this condition, Jenny." Katherine Anderson sat on her knees planting geraniums along the sidewalk leading up to the porch at her daughter's new business venture, Holly Hill Inn.

"Mom, it's just a test weekend. We only have two guests. I'm fine." Jenny pushed soil around her last flower and stood up, brushing the dirt off her hands. "Besides, I'm not due yet for another two months. I've timed things perfectly." Her back did ache though, but that probably had very little to do with her pregnancy. She'd been working long days lately.

Maureen burst out of the house and onto the porch, the screen door slapping hard behind her as it closed. She glanced back. "That is something you need to get fixed. I'll put that on the list for Ben."

Luckily, she had plenty of help today. Wanted or not!

"Ben already knows, Maureen. He's bringing home new hinges today from the hardware."

"Oh, good. I'll check that off my list." Maureen scurried down the steps and to her car. "I'll pick up the groceries on your list I found in the kitchen while I'm heading in to pick up scones from Leslie's Bakery."

"But I wanted to do the grocery shopping...." Her words trailed off as Maureen waved, got in the car, and sped off.

Katherine stood. "Let her. She's almost as OCD as I am about getting things done and list making."

"I've learned that over the past eighteen months, for sure."

They turned as another vehicle made its way up the drive and parked.

Jenny smiled as her husband exited his red pickup truck and headed her way.

"I remembered the hinges," he said, holding them up.

"That's good. Your mother was about to call a repairman."

He rolled his eyes.

Katherine headed for the house. "I'm going to go check on some things in the nursery. I'm sure the baby doesn't have everything he or she needs yet. I wish I knew if this was a boy or a girl..."

She scampered off, probably to make another list, the screen door slapping hard again behind her.

Ben winced. "Did you survive the day?"

"With both your mother and mine? Barely." She laughed.

"I'm so glad to be home." His arms snaked around her waist.

Jenny wrapped hers around his neck. "I'm doubly glad you are here, Mr. Matthews."

He grinned, planted a lingering kiss on Jenny's lips, and then looked to the house. "The place is beautiful."

"Thanks to Elaine and the extra funds she left to us, we've really spruced the place up."

"It's perfect. When do the guests arrive?"

"Friday evening. I can't wait. I've been testing breakfast recipes today. I know it's five o'clock in the afternoon, but want to sample?"

"Show me the way!"

Jenny took Ben's hand and led him up the porch. On the way in, she gave the new sign hanging by the door a tap with her forefingers and smiled. It was her way of saying thank you to Elaine and Harold for their generous wedding gift—a home for Christmas.

HOLLY HILL INN

PROPRIETORS, BEN AND JENNY MATTHEWS

In loving memory of Harold and Elaine Peterson

I hope you enjoyed Ben and Jenny's story. Want to know how life turns out for their children at Holly Hill Inn? Scroll on to read the first chapter of *Miracle at Holly Hill Inn!*

CHAPTER 1—MIRACLE AT HOLLY HILL INN

Present Day

Even the trees sparkle.

Ariana Angelo pushed open her car door and stepped out onto snow-covered pavement. In awe, she scanned her surroundings to take in the quaint New England Main Street lined with Victorian shopfronts—each one decorated to storybook perfection with greenery and red bows, a hefty portion of tinsel and holly, and of course, snow.

The snow was real. None of that fake stuff like back home.

Closing the car door, she moved toward the sidewalk, twirling once, maybe twice, still perusing the most precious Christmas village scene she'd ever before encountered—and that was saying a lot. Christmas was her business, her world— and this town just might be Christmas perfection. She was so glad she'd come.

Stifling the urge to lift her face to the sky and catch a drifting fluffy snowflake on her tongue, she sighed with happiness, eager explore.

Down the street sat the gazebo. She recognized it from pictures she'd seen of the town. It, too, was draped in greenery and ribbons, looking somewhat like a confection sitting atop some sort of pretty Christmas cake—at least one she might bake. It appeared the gazebo was situated within the town square. Beside it was a statue sporting a red scarf, billowing in the brisk breeze. Stepping onto the snow-swept sidewalk, she kept an eye on the structure and wandered a few steps in that direction.

There.

Off to the side of the gazebo stood the town square Christmas tree, proudly displaying gold and silver baubles, ornaments of all colors, and more ribbons—all peeking through fresh snow. The annual Dickens Christmas tree lighting was earlier in the season, and she was sorry she'd missed it—but there was no denying the tree's magnificence.

And, oh? Is that a carousel?

Her insides twittered with glee, bubbling up so rapidly she could barely contain it. She might have let out a quick little giggle.

Pausing her stroll, she spied a colorful sign hanging in the shop window to her right. Her gaze traveled over the shopfront —*Leslie's Bakes & More*—and her tummy started to rumble. Another cup of coffee soon, and perhaps a pastry, would be nice.

Her gaze landed on the red and green sign, again. *Holiday Lighting Event at Holly Hill Inn, Thursday Evening, December 23rd.* With a quick look to the calendar on her digital watch, she smiled. Yes. Today was Wednesday, so the lighting event at the inn was tomorrow—on the eve of Christmas Eve, or Christmas Eve, as she liked to say. Why not stretch out the holiday as long as possible?

Smiling, and immensely happy she'd braved the snowstorm

140

—even against her family's warnings—she felt silly with holiday cheer. The weather had been dicey the day before, delaying her trip into historic Dickens. While she didn't mind getting stuck an extra night at the small New England B&B she'd booked about thirty miles down the road, she was glad the storm had let up enough so she could get to Dickens.

And *bonus!* Due to a cancelation and a matter of happenstance, she had secured a reservation for three nights at the popular Holly Hill Inn, but she was in no hurry to get there. Too much to explore first. Besides, she couldn't check in until late afternoon—so, she had most of the daylight hours left to discover the magic of Dickens at Christmastime.

Dickens just might be the small-town Christmas village of her dreams. She couldn't wait to get pictures and write about it. Her blog readers were going to be so excited.

Reaching into her bag, she pulled out her camera, adjusted the lens, and began walking. As if by magic, the town suddenly teemed with shoppers, milling in and out of the shops, chatting on the sidewalks, and calling out holiday greetings.

Must be getting final shopping done before this storm hits again.

Ariana smiled, dizzy with Christmas excitement, and filled with the holiday spirit. She snapped pictures, chatted with the townsfolk, and gleefully made her way up Main Street, around the square, and down the other side.

Her heart was happy.

It was Christmas.

Nothing could spoil her mood. Absolutely nothing.

Matt Mathews pulled the bottom of his sweater sleeve over the heel of his palm and rubbed out the smudges his breath had just made on the old windowpane. Peering out into the street—perusing the local shoppers and visiting tourists—he sighed. His breath, once again, fogged the glass, so he took one more swipe at it and then turned away.

How many more days until Christmas was over? Too many.

Heading back to his cubby-hole refuge behind the old wooden countertop, tucked into the back of the hardware store, he traveled the center aisle between time-worn, nearly ceiling-high, wooden shelves which housed everything from plumbing and electrical supplies to household cleaners and associated paraphernalia, some small appliances like electric can openers and hand-held mixers, and tools. Lots of tools.

And where there were tools, there were also items that went along with tools—like fence wire, and tape measures, and replacement doorknobs, and cabinet pulls, and such.

Instead of shelves in those areas, there were small wooden drawers—carefully catalogued by his Uncle Wilbur years ago—where one could select nails or screws or bolts or washers, or an assortment of those and other items that a carpenter, or perhaps a crafty person might need.

Yes. Dickens Hardware held all that and more. His family had always strived to provide the town with what they needed, so variety was the mainstay.

What one wouldn't find at Dickens Hardware, however—a store that had been in his family for over a hundred years—was anything to do with Christmas. No tinsel. No trees. No ornaments, holly, wrapping paper, wreaths, or mistletoe.

Ever.

Well, not ever. His mother had stocked quite a bit of holiday cheer and such in the past. But Matt? No. He'd done away with all that years ago.

Christmas was not his thing. It was not his busy season. People weren't shopping for hammers or toilet plungers in

December. They were out for tinsel and wreaths. And truth be known, he'd probably be better off next year to close the store the entire month of December and go someplace warm for a while—someplace where the entire town didn't revel in the idea of the holiday or focus eleven months of the year getting ready for it.

Yes. That is a good idea. Someplace warm.

Matt settled himself on the stool behind the counter, crossed his arms over his chest, and peered out over the store. At some point soon, he should think about walking down the street to grab some lunch—but did he really want to brave the crowd?

Maybe he'd just close the store early and go home. He could always open a can of soup. "Merry Christmas to me."

Ariana impatiently peeked around the line in front of her at Leslie's Bakes & More, trying to get a glimpse at the counter to see what kind of cookies were hiding in front of a gentleman standing there waiting for his sandwich. She tapped her foot, inspecting the quaint interior of the business. Being patient was not her strong suit, so waiting in line for anything was always a challenge. In the meantime, she'd simply busy herself by perusing the Christmas decorations and the people, the confections and pastries, and the deli menu in the small bakery-slash-sandwich shop.

Which was not a bad idea, she surmised, to combine the two types of establishments. The bakery could cater to the breakfast crowd with pastries and coffee earlier in the day, then later, sandwiches and cookies for the lunch crowd. And pie.

Oh, there was pie. She stretched her neck and took a tiny

step to her right to ogle the pie case around the corner from the counter.

Leaning more to her right, she watched the gentleman hiding the cookies step away—*were those Snickerdoodles?*—and the line moved forward.

She took a half-step—but someone darted in front of her, taking her spot in line.

Standing there for a moment, a little befuddled to be perfectly honest, she decided to make the best of it.

"Excuse me." She tapped the man's shoulder. "I'm sure you didn't realize you cut in front of me. I've been standing here for a while. But if you are in a hurry, I'm happy to let you go first. Besides, it's Christmas." She smiled.

He turned and looked at her, mumbled something under his breath, and didn't smile back. "You weren't in line."

"Oh, but I was. Am." Her feet planted, she peered back, not about to move.

He stared back at her with his knit cap pulled down low over his forehead, a shock of brown hair poking out, and his arms crossed tightly over his coat at his chest. "I, also, have been standing in line. You, it appeared, had stepped away and were gawking."

Gawking? "I beg your pardon?"

"Gawking," he replied. "You know, gallerwaggling about. Listlessly wandering. You didn't appear to be standing in line. I thought you were, basically, aimlessly perusing."

Ariana squinted, quickly studying the man. He wasn't an old man. He was, perhaps, a couple of years older than her—but his grumpiness gave off an illusion of being much older—and crotchety. Such a shame. He actually had nice features—high cheekbones, a firm chin, and a scruffy five o'clock shadow that was maybe two days overdue.

She stood a little straighter and set her shoulders. *Forget*

144

about the sexy five o'clock shadow, Ariana. "For the record, I do not gallerwag. Nor do I listlessly wander or aimlessly peruse. I'll have you know that should I ever peruse or wander, I do so with intent. And as to gallerwag? You made that up. It's not a word. Perhaps you meant lollygag."

"No. I meant what I said. Look it up." He turned into the line, showing her his back.

Not to be dismissed, Ariana poked him on the shoulder again with her forefinger. "I actually don't carry a dictionary with me. Besides, words are my business and that is not one."

He shrugged. "Got your phone? Google it." He gave her a backward glance.

"I most certainly will." Reaching for her purse, and her phone, she paused, then looked at the back of his head. "Later. You are intentionally distracting me."

He half-turned. "You were already distracted."

Sidling up next to him, she made eye contact. Just for the record, she noted to herself, they were deep brown and...well, right now, they were sort of probing hers. "I'll have you know I was not distracted. I'm a writer. I observe things. You came from nowhere and simply cut in line in front of me."

"Not exactly correct." He took a step forward with the moving line. "I've been standing behind you for a few minutes. You stepped out of line, so...."

"I most certainly did not step out of line." She countered his step and took another one ahead of him.

"Are you cutting in front of me?"

"Just reclaiming my place in line."

"Oh, no. I'm next."

In exasperation, Ariana clenched her fists and glared at him. "My God. What a Scrooge." She thought she heard someone off to the side snicker. Glancing that way, she realized they'd become the center of attention.

Great.

He made direct eye contact again with her, leaned in a bit, and then said loudly and very clearly, "Bah. Humbug."

"Next." The young man behind the counter called out.

Swiftly turning, Ariana blurted, "Medium black coffee and three of those cookies." She pointed to the Snickerdoodles.

"The usual, Tom," the man said simultaneously.

Tom eyed them both.

Ariana refused to look at the man standing next to her. *The usual?* A local. Suddenly, her impression of the town was slightly soured, but she was not going to let that sway her.

"Coming right up," Tom said.

"Thank you," Ariana and the man said in unison.

She glanced at him. He looked down at her.

Ariana broke eye contact and looked ahead, waiting for her coffee and cookies. After several long seconds of drumming her fingertips on the counter, she sighed when he set a cup of coffee and a white bag of cookies in front of her.

"Four dollars and ninety-eight cents, ma'am."

She opened her wallet.

"Put it on mine, Tom," the man next to her said.

Immediately, she protested. "Oh, no. I'll get it. But thank you."

"My pleasure." He nodded to Tom.

"I mean, I'll take care of my own bill."

He peered down. "Welcome to Dickens. I hope you enjoyed your stay. Be careful on your way out of town."

Ariana gathered her coffee and cookies, then looked back up to the guy. "Well, thank you, but I'm not leaving. In fact, I just got here and am planning to stay for a few days. I appreciate the warm welcome." The saccharin sweet smile she tossed him almost made her nauseous. But no matter, she decided right then and there, she was not going to let this

single, unhappy incident spoil her mood—or her impression of
Dickens.

"Merry Christmas," she said, turning to leave.

He grunted something.

Ariana paused, her gaze straight ahead, and headed out of
the shop.

Get **Miracle at Holly Hill Inn** at your favorite bookseller,
today!

And also look for **The Last Christmas at Holly Hill Inn**
coming October 2021.

DO YOU GET MY INSIDER NEWS?

Be the first to get the latest news about my books—new releases, free ebooks, sales and discounts, sneak peeks, and exclusive content! Just add your email address at this link: https://www.maddiejames.net/p/newsletter.html
Bonus! I'll send you a FREE Six-Book Boxed Set for signing up.

Maddie James writes to silence the people in her head—if only they wouldn't all talk at once!

From flirty contemporary romance to darker erotic titles—often mixed with a dash of suspense or a hint of paranormal—Maddie pens stories that frequently blend a variety of romantic sub-genres. The happily-ever-after, of course, is non-negotiable.

Affaire de Coeur says, "James shows a special talent for traditional romance," and *RT Book Reviews* claims, "James deftly combines romance and suspense." Maddie is the award-winning author of over fifty titles of fiction—from short stories to novels—and a Top 100 Amazon Bestselling Author.

Learn more at http://www.maddiejames.org.